VANISHED VILLAGE

He made camp at the site, puzzled at himself for doing so. He built a fire in a hollow, where it could not be seen from the surrounding plain. After coffee, he wandered along the bank of the Little Dry. Now the place where the tipis once stood was empty, snowy ground. His father and mother had died here, and for a while he wondered who they had been, how old or how young. Had his father been a warrior, chief, or medicine man? Had his mother been beautiful?

The answers had been in this place once but were here no more. It was a lonely, forgotten spot, living only in the minds of those who had come to kill twenty years before. And in Johnny's mind.

But the faceless, voiceless men and women who had been murdered were crying out for vengeance after all the years. **They were reaching from the grave for their killers, one by one . . .**

⊘ Signet Brand Western

Other SIGNET Westerns You'll Want to Read

THE GUILTY GUNS

by

Lewis B. Patten

Ⓢ
A SIGNET BOOK

NEW AMERICAN LIBRARY

TIMES MIRROR

Copyright © 1963 by Lewis B. Patten

Published by Arrangement with the author

SIGNET TRADEMARK REG. U.S. PAT. OFF. AND FOREIGN COUNTRIES
REGISTERED TRADEMARK—MARCA REGISTRADA
HECHO EN CHICAGO, U.S.A.

SIGNET, SIGNET CLASSICS, MENTOR, PLUME AND MERIDIAN BOOKS
are published by The New American Library, Inc.,
1301 Avenue of the Americas, New York, New York 10019

FIRST SIGNET PRINTING, JANUARY, 1979

1 2 3 4 5 6 7 8 9

PRINTED IN THE UNITED STATES OF AMERICA

CHAPTER 1

THE TEN rode silently through the pre-dawn chill of early morning, their collars turned up around their ears, their hands gloved, their breath visible in the frosty air, and stopped their horses just below the crest of a small ridge as gray began to streak the autumn sky.

Bradford Gore, towering ponderously in his saddle, turned his shaggy head and spoke in a voice that was tight with strain. "Ready?"

Beeson coughed, then said in a choked, scared voice, "I don't know, Brad. I don't know if...."

"Oh for Christ's sake, don't turn yellow now! They had a beef on a spit down there last night. I saw it myself. And it ain't just that one, either. They kill a beef two or three times every goddam week. My beef. Yours too, Beeson. But if you figure it's up to you to keep them in meat...."

Hunsicker broke in, "No by God!" His thick, Germanic voice made the word sound like "Gott." "I say we go ahead. Just like we planned."

Gore looked at the rest of them. "How about it? Hell, we talked this over. We decided. The law ain't going to help. So it's up to us."

Nobody spoke. Gore said angrily, "We ain't got all day. I'm going to call your names. When I do, just say whether you want to go ahead or not. I'm damned if I want anybody sayin' this was all my idea." He waited a moment and then said heavily, almost threateningly, "Chavez?"

"Si."

"Le Gros?"

"Yes. I think this is something we mus' do. I . . ."

"Never mind the speech. Hunsicker?"

"Ya."

"Jake?"

Fahnstock nodded his head, staring at the ground.

"De Loach?"

"All right. But. . . ."

"God damn it, yes or no?"

"Yes." There was surly resentment in De Loach's voice.

"Carlin?" Gore's voice was beginning to sound like that of a sergeant calling off the roll.

"No. I'm going back. I'm damned. . . ."

Gore said softly, "Floyd, you're just hangin' on by the skin of your teeth. You can't afford to lose a single steer. We been helpin' you and we'll go on helpin' you, but you got to help us, too."

"Well. . . ."

"Good!" Gore said. "I knew you'd see it that way. Tony?"

Barletta nodded violently. "Do we got to stand here jawin' about it all day? Let's go get it done!"

"Karl?"

"Sure." There was an angry bitterness in this man's voice. "Sure, let's go down an' slaughter 'em. The sons-of-bitches are stealing food from us. Only while we're doing it, let's don't remember that it was us who butchered their buffalo. That's different anyhow."

Gore said angrily, "Shut up! Nobody made you come along. Don't get high and mighty about it now."

It was a moment before Karl replied. When he did, his tone betrayed his knowledge that Gore's accusation was true. He said with self-condemning bitterness, "All right. I'll shut up. I'll even go down there and help because I haven't got the guts to try and make it on my place without your help. Because maybe I know that, right or wrong, there are times when people have to stand together. Oh hell! . . ." He subsided, muttering to himself.

"That leaves Beeson, then. You still want to back out, Roy? You want everyone to think you're yellow and willin' to let 'em do your dirty work for you?"

Beeson said softly, "You're a bastard, Gore, a dirty, murderin' bastard. You're not doing this because you have to. You're going to enjoy it."

Gore's horse moved with unexpected suddenness. The big man's hands went out and yanked Beeson brutally from his saddle. Beeson thumped on the ground with a surprised grunt. When he got up, Gore was waiting for him. His fists made meaty, sodden sounds as they struck Beeson's face.

Beeson never made a sound. He fell and lay still. Breathing hard, Gore turned. "We'll leave him here until we're through."

Nobody spoke after that. Gore mounted, his breath wheezing rapidly in and out of his massive chest. He said harshly, "Come on."

He whirled his horse and sank his spurs. The others followed suit. Some of them drew revolvers from holsters at their sides. Others yanked rifles from saddle scabbards.

Ahead of them, in a wide, shallow draw split in the center by a small stream, an Indian village slept in the early dawn.

Dogs began to bark. The sound of galloping hoofs was a dull thunder that brought blanketed and half-naked Indians through the tipi flaps. A cry of alarm was raised, its words unintelligible, but its meaning unmistakable.

The light was stronger now. Gore's horse sailed over a small wash and the others followed suit. One man raised his revolver and fired.

Gore cursed him, then gestured to right and left. The men fanned out into a line, the intervals between them growing to about twenty feet.

Seventeen lodges. Between seventy-five and a hundred people. Maybe twenty men.

Only a hundred yards now separated the galloping horsemen from the nearest lodge. It dwindled rapidly to fifty yards. Gore raised his revolver, sighted carefully, and dropped a squaw trying to reach the doubtful shelter of the stream bank.

Then they were in the midst of the tipis, their guns volleying rapidly like strings of firecrackers on the Fourth of July.

A boy, perhaps two, ran screaming from one of the tipi flaps directly into Gore's path. Struck by a flying hoof, he was flung aside, to fall on his back, eyes closed, blood oozing from a forehead wound.

A young squaw ran screaming to snatch him up but was hit by a bullet in the back before she could. She fell, one of her outstretched hands just touching him.

A few tomahawks were thrown, a few arrows shot. One of these took Floyd Carlin in the arm. A tomahawk knocked Ernst Hunsicker from his saddle.

The horsemen swept through the village, reloaded and swept back through again. They dismounted after the second sweep and went in on foot, using their rifle butts instead of bullets for mopping up.

The sun poked above the eastern plain, its rays warming and bright. It shone starkly on the dead in the village of Bear Claw on the banks of a tiny stream to be later known as Little Dry Creek or, "The Little Dry."

The white men rode away, Carlin with a blood-soaked bandage on his arm. Hunsicker with a growing lump on the right side of his forehead. They left behind only the dead, and one other they thought was dead, the two-year-old boy that had been knocked unconscious by a horse's hoof.

Tom Ormsby was a squat, bull-shouldered, bow-legged man of thirty. Like most men, he wore a beard, but he kept it neatly clipped beneath the long, curving, cavalry-style mustache that adorned his upper lip.

From a distance of several miles he heard the faint popping of gunfire, and stopped, frowning, to listen. At first the thought occurred to him that someone had found a herd of buffalo. Almost immediately he realized how impossible that was. The buffalo were gone. He hadn't seen a single one for several months.

He turned his horse toward the sounds and had ridden for almost a mile before they ceased. After that, there was complete silence on the plain. The sun poked above the eastern horizon and climbed deliberately across a cloudless sky.

Ormsby was not a timid man, but neither could he be called a fool. He approached with extreme caution, using each natural bit of concealment that offered itself—a dry wash—a knoll standing between himself and the place toward which he rode.

It was, perhaps, two hours after he had first heard the shots that he crested a small rise and stared into the wide, shallow ravine in which the Indian village lay.

Dogs began almost immediately to bark at him, but other than that of the dogs, he saw no movement at all. No human stirred. The Indians lay about on the ground as though they were asleep. Ormsby knew, with a sick, empty feeling in his chest, that they were all dead.

He sat there, unbelieving, for several minutes. A breeze blowing toward him from the village apparently carried to his horse a smell of blood, for the animal began to prance nervously. He rolled his eyes and laid back his ears.

Ormsby held him with an inflexible hand. Slowly, he began a circle of the village, well aware that if any Indians remained alive they would kill him without hesitation, believing him to be one of the attackers come back to make sure that all were dead or to collect souvenirs.

He found the wide-spaced trails of the white men going in. He found their overlapping trails coming out again, this time in a bunch. He completed his circle of the village, then sat unmoving on the knoll again and watched some more.

He was sick with horror at the brutality of it. Best thing for him to do, he thought, was to ride away without ever going close. He didn't want his horse's tracks found inside that dead village.

Besides, he doubted if he could do anyone any good by riding in. They were dead. Even if one or two remained alive, they would probably die before he could get help for them.

He turned and started to ride away, then froze, listening, holding his horse motionless with an iron-tight grasp on the reins. For a second time he heard it, a sound understandable, exactly the same in any language. It was the terror-stricken crying of a child.

Ormsby turned his horse back toward the village. With an eerie crawling in his spine, he urged the animal along reluctantly. A child crying that lustily could not be badly hurt. And he couldn't leave it here to die.

Wary, he approached, his hand never far from the grip of his gun. He kept glancing to right and left, watching for movement in the bodies he passed. He would shoot instantly and without hesitation if any of them threatened him. There would be no time for explanations and he didn't intend to be killed himself.

But nothing moved. The frightened crying continued. He rode slowly up and down the village streets, searching for the source of the sound, which at one time seemed to come from one direction, at another from a different one.

He saw the child at last, caught a glimpse of him running behind a weathered buffalo-hide tipi.

He swung to the ground, dropped his reins and ran.

Scared, the kid might be, he thought. But that hadn't impaired his ability to run. It was like trying to catch a cottontail in a cornfield. Ormsby ran until his breath came from his chest like the sound of a bellows. He dove at the boy at last, caught him by one ankle.

The boy, who could not have been more than two, doubled at once and sank his sharp white teeth into Ormsby's hand. Ormsby whacked him on the side of the head reflexively, because the bite went deep.

Half stunned, the boy was still long enough for Ormsby to rise with him clutched against his chest. Then he began to kick. He was no longer crying, but was saving his breath for his struggles with the white man who had captured him.

Ormsby grunted, "You damn little redskin, quit kickin' me. I ain't fixin' to hurt you. Damn it, you want me to leave you here?"

The boy kicked harder, but he made no sound.

He was dressed only in a buckskin shirt. His feet were bare. His hair, not yet long enough to braid, fell halfway to his shoulders and was blue-black and straight.

Ormsby reached his horse. He squatted beside the animal and turned the boy around. He supposed his bearded face would further terrify the boy, but he had to try something. He looked straight and earnestly into the child's wide brown eyes. He said as soothingly as though he were speaking to a frightened horse, "Whoa there youngster. I ain't goin' to hurt you none. I ain't one of them that shot up the place. I heard the shots an' come to see what was happenin'. You can't stay here. There's nobody left alive to look after you an' you sure as hell can't make it on your own. So you just come along with me an' I'll look after you, leastwise until I can find someone of your own kind to take over the job for me. All right?"

There must have been some hypnotic quality in his soothing voice. It was certain the child could not have understood his words. But perhaps he did understand the compassion, the sincerity, the pity in Ormsby's eyes and voice. He stared unblinkingly into Ormsby's eyes but stopped clawing and kicking and stopped trying to get away.

Ormsby smiled at him. "Good. Now let's you an' me get up on this here horse and get the hell out of here before somebody shows up and accuses old Tom Ormsby of havin' had a hand in it. All right?"

The boy continued to stare at him disconcertingly. The terror in his eyes seemed less.

Tom Ormsby put the boy astride the horse, then swung up behind him. He reined the horse away.

The boy struggled briefly and cried out in a lost and haunted way, words that Ormsby could not understand. He held the child more firmly until he stopped.

This way, they cleared the edge of the murdered village and rode across the plain in the clean morning sunlight. Ten minutes later they were only a speck in the emptiness. Half an hour later they had disappeared.

CHAPTER 2

Tom Ormsby watched Johnny ride down Main, a strangely worried expression in his eyes. He was older now. There was a heavy shading of gray in his hair. His beard was gone, but the old-style, cavalry mustache remained and it, too, was liberally salted with gray.

It had been a long time since the massacre on the Little Dry, he thought. Twenty years this month. That would make Johnny twenty-two.

Thick-bodied and strong, even at fifty, he stood firmly rooted to the street like a giant cottonwood. There was a star pinned to his vest. Another was pinned to Johnny's shirt. Tom had been sheriff of Pawnee County for fifteen years. Johnny had been his deputy for three, ever since he turned nineteen.

He wondered, sometimes, how smart he had been to tell Johnny about the massacre on the Little Dry, though the boy had seemed to take it well. Still, you never knew. Johnny was white in environment, in education, but he looked Indian and maybe he thought Indian too. Tom would know when he got back. He had deliberately sent Johnny out alone after Norman De Loach, aware that Johnny knew De Loach had participated in the massacre. Now all he could do was wait, to see if Johnny brought De Loach back to town alive.

Maybe it was cruel to put Johnny to a test this way. But Tom Ormsby had to know. For his own peace of mind, for the future, he had to know whether Johnny was a Cheyenne bent on vengeance for a wrong perpetrated years before, or whether he was a conscientious sheriff's deputy who could be trusted to do his job without letting personal considerations enter into it.

Johnny rode out at a steady trot, knowing the trail would be long and that if he didn't save his horse's strength he would never reach its end.

He was a tall young man, with the strong, muscular build of a Cheyenne brave. He rode loosely and well, as comfortable on a horse as he was any other place.

His hair was black, clipped fairly short and covered with a shapeless broad-brimmed hat. His eyes were brown, sometimes fierce, sometimes laughing, sometimes soft. His high cheekbones made his cheeks seem hollow and his nose was straight and prominent above a mouth inclined to thinness and a chin that jutted firmly beneath it.

He wore a blue shirt, faded at the armpits and down the back by sweat, a pair of tight wool pants and high-heeled boots with spurs. Tied behind his saddle was a blanket roll, denim jacket, a yellow slicker and a sack of provisions and cooking gear.

A holstered revolver sagged from a well-filled cartridge belt near his right hand. A carbine was stuffed into a saddle boot. His horse was a black, with three white stockings and a blazed face.

De Loach's trail was easy to follow because of the speed at which the man's horse had been traveling. Johnny left the town behind as the early morning sun climbed across the sky, his eyes intent but showing a troubled quality too.

He knew De Loach had participated in the Little Dry massacre. De Loach may even have been the one who killed his mother and father. He wondered how he would feel when he caught up with the man, how much he would be thinking of revenge for the massacre and how much he would be thinking that De Loach was simply a killer who had shot an unarmed man in the Buckhorn saloon last night and who had to be brought in for trial.

Unconsciously he turned his head and looked behind, though the town of Box Elder was out of sight. His thoughts still saw old Tom standing there, thick legs spread, hat pulled low over his sharp blue eyes against the slanting, bright rays of the morning sun.

He found himself imagining what it had been like that morning twenty years ago. His mind saw the Indian village sleeping peacefully on the bank of the Little Dry. He saw the ten, sitting their horses on a low bluff, staring down.

He seemed to hear the crackling shots and the cries of the wounded and dying. Yet no firm memory came back to him. He had been too young.

Tom Ormsby hadn't seen the men, or tracked them either. He had pieced together information, knowing who lived in the area, knowing all of them well. In the end he had known the name of every man who had participated in the attack.

And Johnny knew them too, from Bradford Gore, who had been mentioned recently as a possible candidate for governor, to Norman De Loach, who in recent years had been nothing but a drunk.

Funny. Maybe something was wrong with him. Maybe he ought to be thirsting for revenge now that he was grown. But he wasn't. The massacre had taken place twenty years before. It was over and done.

Besides, it was likely that every one of the participants had paid for his part in it, each in his own private hell of guilt. And each would probably go on paying until he died. No reason why Johnny should cut that natural process short.

Two or three miles from town, De Loach's horse had stopped. There were boot tracks on the ground, showing where De Loach had dismounted. But the trail went on, though at a moderated pace.

Johnny followed it patiently throughout the day. That night, he camped at dusk when it became too dark to trail. He made coffee over a small fire, fried bacon and then potatoes in the grease. Afterward he laid down and covered himself with his blankets. He stared thoughtfully at the stars.

The tracks had indicated an increasing pace all through the afternoon. By now, he guessed, De Loach would be cold sober and would be getting a case of the shakes. He would need a drink and need it bad. There was only one town over this way where he could get one and that was Collinsville.

Johnny got up suddenly. To hell with slavishly

following trail. If his hunch was wrong, if he didn't turn De Loach up in Collinsville, he could still get back here before dawn and take up the trail where he'd left off. All he'd have lost was a night's sleep.

He packed his gear and saddled his horse. He swung to the saddle and rode east. He let his horse travel at a rolling lope, slowing him only when it became apparent the animal was breathing hard. In air cool with the coming of fall, the miles fell rapidly behind.

It was almost eleven when he saw the lights of Collinsville come into view. The place could scarcely be called a town, he thought. It had only one street, dusty when it was dry and muddy whenever it rained. There were buildings on both sides of the street, a hotel, two saloons, a livery stable, a blacksmith shop. There were half a dozen residences as well, ranging from a one-room sod shack to a two-story frame. There was a restaurant too . . . Johnny grinned to himself. A girl ran that restaurant. . . . But she might be married by now. He hadn't seen her since mid-summer and a girl like that didn't go unclaimed long.

Gerda Hoffman, a German girl with yellow hair that was like silk, skin as flawless and white as fine china, smiling, and sometimes mocking lips and eyes as blue as a summer sky. A girl that treated Johnny like any man, not like a Cheyenne Indian the way most others did.

He rode in with only a penetrating glance at each saloon, and dismounted at the door of the restaurant, which was half a block north of the hotel. He tied his horse, stretched, then went inside.

She glanced up and there was no mistaking the genuine welcome her eyes held for him. She smiled instantly and cried, "Johnny! Johnny Ormsby! I was beginning to wonder if something had happened to you."

He grinned. "I got lonesome. I got so I just didn't figure I could live any longer without seeing you."

Gerda's full lips became mocking. "Blarney. Are you Irish or Cheyenne?"

"You'd bring blarney out of a wooden Indian." He crossed the room and went behind the counter. He put a big hand on either side of her slim waist and lifted her up. She squirmed and kicked, laughing, but she didn't turn her head away when he planted a firm kiss on her mouth. Her arms went around his neck.

After a moment he put her down, backed out from behind the counter and sat down on one of the stools. She stared at him closely for several moments, her smile fading. "Who are you after, Johnny? You didn't come 'way over here just to see me."

"I did too."

"Who, Johnny?"

He said, "De Loach. He killed an unarmed man in the Buckhorn last night."

"And you trailed him here?"

"Not all the way. I came on, figuring he was heading here. By now I think he needs a drink."

"He did, Johnny. Bad enough to kill for it."

"What are you talking about?"

"Somebody caught old Nels Rickstrew as he

was heading home about dusk tonight. Clubbed him and took the bottle Nels had bought. Got away before anybody could recognize him."

"And Nels is dead?"

"Yes Johnny. He's dead."

She turned her back, went into the kitchen to get him a cup of coffee. Over her shoulder she called, "Hungry?"

"Uh uh. Coffee's fine." He watched her slim, straight form. She was rather small by comparison to himself but there was nothing weak in her.

Why didn't he push a little more, he wondered. He wanted Gerda and sometimes he got the feeling that she wouldn't tell him no, in spite of his Indian blood, but he'd never pushed it much.

Hell, maybe he would. Maybe when he took De Loach back, he'd get Tom to let him take a couple of weeks off. He'd come over here to Collinsville and camp in Gerda's restaurant and find out if she'd say yes to him.

She came back with the coffee and set it down in front of him. Her eyes met his and her skin turned briefly pink. He said, "Mind reader."

"Your mind isn't very hard to read." She refused to meet his eyes.

"You're a pretty woman. What would you say if I asked you to marry me?"

She glanced up quickly. Her face had lost its color and her eyes were wide. "Are you asking, Johnny?"

"I might, after I've courted you proper for a spell. Would you go live in a tipi with me?"

"Johnny, don't talk like that. It doesn't sound like you."

He fingered the star on his shirt. "Guess not."

He was thinking that without the star things would be different for him. Nobody would have to accept him then. He had the star, though, and with it a place in the community. He was going to keep them both, at least as long as Tom Ormsby was sheriff. He was damned if anyone was going to make a blanket Indian out of him just because his skin was dark.

But he knew something else as well. If he married Gerda and took her home to Box Elder with him, the people there would make it hard for her, just as they'd always made it hard for him.

The time would come, of course, when an Indian would be accepted without prejudice. Trouble was, not enough years had passed for either side to forget the conflict that had raged between them.

He drank his coffee slowly, talking to Gerda, and when the cup was empty, she refilled it for him. By the time he had finished this cup, it was midnight. He said, "Walk you home?"

"All right."

She banked the fire in the stove and blew out the lamps. She followed Johnny out, locking the door behind her.

The air was crisp with coming fall. A few dry leaves rustled along the street. There was a pleasant odor of woodsmoke and a hint of frost in the air. She took his arm and walked with rapid steps beside him, along the street to the hotel.

Inside the dreary lobby he said, "I'll take De Loach back and then I'm going to ask Tom for a couple of weeks off. I'm going to camp over here until you say yes."

Her eyes rested disconcertingly on his face.

"Then you're going to give me a chance to say yes?"

He said, "Don't be so brazen. You might scare me off."

"I don't think you scare very easily."

"Maybe I scare easier than you think. Maybe it scares me to think of anybody treating you like a squaw."

"Johnny, stop it!"

He shrugged. "Good night."

"Good night, Johnny." She crossed the lobby and climbed the stairs. Johnny walked to the desk and paid for a room. Afterward he went back outside and led his horse to the livery barn. Returning to the hotel, he climbed the stairs to his room, went in and went to bed. He slept.

CHAPTER 3

HE AWOKE, from long established habit, as dawn was beginning to streak the eastern sky. He got up, instantly awake, and dressed. He washed in the cold water kept in the pitcher in his room and ran a short comb through his black hair. He put on his hat, belted on his gun and went down the stairs, through the deserted lobby, and into the crisp morning air.

No lights showed anywhere in the town. He wished he had some coffee but knew he could not afford to wait for it.

He saddled his horse at the livery barn and led him out. Then he mounted and began a half-circle along the eastern edge of town, searching for De Loach's trail.

The sky grew lighter slowly. After about ten minutes of looking, he found the trail, the same trail he had followed out of Box Elder the day before.

If De Loach had gotten a bottle from the man he'd killed he would probably have stopped somewhere last night, either because he was too drunk to ride, or because he wanted to drink it leisurely. He would have a monstrous hangover this morning. He'd be mean and unpredictable, which would make Johnny's task of taking him alive no easier.

The sun poked above the plain and began its steady climb across the sky. A bank of gray, low-lying clouds hung on the northern horizon, forecasting a storm which would probably strike today.

The trail continued steadily eastward until mid-morning and then it stopped. Johnny found the place where the horse had been tied to a clump of brush. He followed De Loach's unsteady tracks to a small ravine, where he found the empty whisky bottle and the cork nearby.

He rode out again along the trail, which no longer traveled in a direct line east. The horse seemed to be making his own way and it was erratic and plainly slow.

Johnny's eyes scanned each bit of cover carefully. Chances were good, he thought, that he'd be overtaking De Loach fairly soon. He hoped the man would be passed out someplace, sleeping off the effects of the liquor he had consumed. But he knew there was a good chance De Loach would still be conscious, waiting for him behind some rock or clump of brush, rifle leveled.

He shrugged fatalistically. That was a chance a lawman took every time he trailed a criminal. But he doubted if De Loach's aim would be too good. De Loach's hangover would improve the chances that his first shot, at least, would miss.

The grass underfoot was dry and rustled under his horse's hoofs. A band of antelope watched him pass curiously from a nearby knoll. And suddenly he became aware that he was no longer stirring up flocks of small birds. He hadn't seen a rabbit for several miles.

That was a tip-off in itself. De Loach must have

passed through here only minutes before. And if Johnny was that close to him, it was probable that the ambush was not very far ahead.

His vigilance increased. His eyes shifted back and forth, from rock to rock, from brush clump to brush clump.

He was approaching a bluff, with steep sides and a shelf of rimrock at the top. At the bottom of it was a deep ravine.

He tensed in his saddle, no longer watching the landscape, instead watching his horse's head. Suddenly the animal's ears pricked forward. He sidestepped nervously.

The shot came, first as a puff of smoke from the lip of the ravine, next as a report that reverberated from the rimrock behind the marksman. But Johnny was ready and left his horse in a single, swift movement. He disappeared behind a clump of low, yellow-flowered rabbit brush, rifle in hand and poked out in front of him.

He remained very still for what seemed an eternity, hoping De Loach would not get the idea of killing his horse. At last he yelled, "De Loach! It's Johnny Ormsby. Throw out your gun and come out after it."

There was silence for several moments. Johnny yelled, "De Loach?"

The voice that answered was thick and hoarse. "To hell with you, you dirty redskin! If you want to kill me you'll have to come after me!"

Johnny's clenching jaw was the only indication of resentment at the epithet. He yelled, "Who said I wanted to kill you? You'll get a trial."

"Hah! Funny, ain't you? You know damned good and well I was with the bunch that wiped out your village twenty years ago. I ain't fool enough to think you've forgotten it."

Johnny yelled, "That was twenty years ago."

"Maybe it was, but I've thought about it every goddam day and you have too."

Johnny looked around helplessly. There was no way he could get closer without exposing himself. He called, "As far as I'm concerned, it's over with. If I'd wanted to kill you, don't you think I'd have done it before this?"

"You never had a chance like this before." The voice assumed a pleading quality. "It wasn't me that headed up that bunch. I went along because Brad made me go. I swear it, Johnny. I swear that's true."

"All right. I believe you. Now come on out."

He got no answer, unless De Loach's bullets could be called that. But he did get an unexpected break. The rapid volley from De Loach's gun apparently frightened his horse into pulling loose. He came up out of the ravine and trotted nervously away. Johnny drew a careful bead on the horse's neck and fired. The horse dropped and was completely still.

Johnny shouted, "You'll never make it now, De Loach. Your horse is dead. Come on out while you've still got a chance."

De Loach's head and rifle barrel poked up over the lip of the ravine. Johnny saw that the rifle was lined out toward his own horse, behind him and on his left.

He fired a bullet directly in front of De Loach and it showered the man with dirt. Both head and rifle disappeared. For several long moments all was silent and nothing moved.

Nervously Johnny looked to right and left along the lip of the ravine. He didn't want to walk all the way back to Collinsville and he would if De Loach managed to get his horse.

Unexpectedly, he saw De Loach's rifle come up out of the ravine. De Loach shouted, "All right. You win. You got my eyes so goddamn full of dirt. . . ."

The man came climbing out of the ravine, his hands rubbing his eyes. He stumbled toward Johnny helplessly.

Johnny stood up, his rifle pointing at the ground. He said, "Toss your revolver on the ground."

"Sure." De Loach fumbled blindly for the gun.

Too late, Johnny saw that the man was feigning blindness, that there was no dirt in his eyes at all. Too late, he saw how fast that gun came out, how unerringly it lined itself on his chest.

He flung himself aside, felt the burn of De Loach's bullet tearing along the muscles of his upper arm. If he hadn't moved. . . .

He rolled desperately. De Loach's gun roared again and this bullet tore up a shower of dirt less than a foot from his head.

He dropped his rifle, knowing he could never bring it to bear in time. Still rolling, he snatched for his own revolver, praying it had not been lost in the fall.

He felt his hand close over its grips as De Loach's third bullet tore into the heel of his boot, the impact numbing his leg all the way to the knee. Still rolling, he yanked out his revolver and thumbed the hammer. He froze for an instant,

23

while he lined the gun on De Loach, and fired almost instantly.

De Loach fired a fourth time as Johnny's bullet struck, but the gun was deflected by the shock. The man took an unsteady step back away from Johnny and his gun fell from his hand. He stared at Johnny. "I knew you would," he croaked. "I knew...."

Johnny got to his feet. De Loach stood there swaying, staring at him with accusing eyes. Johnny said angrily, "Damn you, did you give me any choice? What am I supposed to do, stand still and let you kill me?"

De Loach didn't answer. His eyes were glazed. He pitched forward and fell at Johnny's feet, his breathing stilled, his face buried in the dust.

Johnny pulled the empty automatically from his gun and replaced it with a fresh cartridge from his belt. He shoved the gun into its holster, stepped over to De Loach and stared down at him. Then he turned, retrieved his rifle and went after his horse, limping because the heel of his right boot was gone.

He hadn't wanted to kill De Loach. He knew Tom woudn't approve of it. But hell, he hadn't had a choice.

He returned, leading the horse, and loaded De Loach's limp body behind the saddle, afterward tying it down. He picked up De Loach's guns, mounted, then turned the horse westward again. He supposed the whole damned town would say he had killed De Loach for revenge. But it wasn't true. At least Johnny himself knew it wasn't true.

In mid-morning, low, gray, moisture-laden

clouds obscured the sun and began to drive swiftly past overhead, moving from north to south. At noon, it began to snow, the first flakes hard and stinging cores of ice that did not fall but pelted almost horizontally against everything moving in the street.

Tom Ormsby stood in the window of the sheriff's office and scowled at the growing fury of the storm. Not that he was worried about Johnny. The boy could take care of himself in a storm. But if he hadn't already caught up with De Loach, he would lose him now for sure.

He was a bit startled to see a group of men approaching from downstreet where the Buckhorn saloon was, barely visible through the snow. They were clad in heavy mackinaws and sheepskins, with the collars turned up around their ears. Several of them had scarfs or bandannas tied over their ears underneath their hats.

The door swung open, admitting a blast of cold air and a cloud of snow. The men came in.

Now, with recognition, a feeling of deep uneasiness touched the sheriff's mind. This was the group of which De Loach had once been a part. This was the group that had raided the village on the Little Dry and massacred its inhabitants twenty years before.

Fidel Chavez, grizzled and graying now and grown heavier with the years. Rene Le Gros, thin and sharp-faced, and inclined to tirades. Ernst Hunsicker, bald and fat. Jake Fahnstock, wearing gold-rimmed glasses and peering nervously through them as though he couldn't see.

Bradford Gore was missing, but Floyd Carlin was here, and Roy Beeson, and Tony Barletta, who ran the barber shop. Karl Asbury came in last, thoughtful, calm, and a little bit ashamed.

Hunsicker spoke for the group. "Johnny come back yet?"

Ormsby shook his head.

"You were a fool to send him out alone. He'll kill De Loach, and that'll give him a taste for blood. Our blood. You should've gone with him. Once a redskin gets a taste of revenge. . . ."

"Johnny's not interested in revenge. If he wanted it, don't you think he'd have done something about it a long time before this?"

"He ain't very old. I've seen the way he looks at me, like he'd cut my goddam heart out if he could."

"That could be your conscience, Ernst."

Hunsicker's fat face turned red with anger. His tiny eyes, peering from between the rolls of fat above and below them, were as hard as those of a boar. "Don't get smart with me, Tom. You're an elected official and it was us that put you where you are."

Anger now touched Tom Ormsby's eyes. He said, "Last election I pulled six hundred and seven votes in this county. I'm only looking at eight. You go straight to hell, Ernst."

Asbury broke in placatingly, "We're not criticizing you, Tom. Not exactly. Thing is, too many people around here remember the Indian troubles. They don't like to see Johnny wearing that deputy's star."

"He's been a damn good deputy. Best one this county ever had. He can trail like a bloodhound and he ain't afraid of anything. I sent him out alone after De Loach on purpose because I knew what the bunch of you would say. I wanted to show you how goddam wrong you were. All nine of you have been pussyfooting around town ever since I made Johnny my deputy, making sly talk about his Indian blood. It hasn't been Johnny or anything he's done that made you talk that way, either. It was your own stinking, guilty consciences. You rode into that village twenty years ago and butchered those people because they stole a steer. You've lived with it ever since and just because the law never made you pay doesn't mean you haven't paid. But I'm warning you: don't touch Johnny. Don't think you can ease your consciences by getting rid of him. I'll personally see to it that the man who kills him hangs. And I'll know exactly where to look."

"We never said anything about killing him. We just don't want him wearing a deputy's star, lordin' it over us...."

"He never lorded it over anybody. Maybe he was born in a tipi. Maybe his skin is dark. But he's been educated like a white and raised like one. He don't know any more of the Cheyenne tongue than I do and I taught him that." He paused furiously for breath, then roared, "Get out of here, the whole damn bunch of you! Johnny'll be back tonight or first thing tomorrow. He'll have De Loach with him too—alive. De Loach will go to trial."

He glared around at the faces of the men confronting him. Not one of them would meet his eyes. Muttering to themselves, they turned, opened the door and shuffled out into the storm.

Tom kicked it shut behind Fahnstock, last to go outside. He turned and angrily replenished the

27

fire in the stove. He kicked a piece of firewood halfway across the room.

Elections were coming up next year and he hadn't helped his chance of re-election any just a few moments before. All eight of the men who had just gone out were influential men. They could swing a lot of votes.

But he didn't care. He was sick of seeing Johnny treated like an outcast. He would bet his life that Johnny would never seek revenge against any one of those guilty of the massacre on the Little Dry. All Johnny wanted was to be let alone.

And yet, in spite of his self-assurances, a little core of doubt hung uneasily in the back of his mind.

CHAPTER 4

CARRYING DOUBLE, hampered by driving snow and by slick ground underfoot, Johnny's horse plodded westward toward the town of Box Elder. Johnny ducked his head uncomfortably against the stinging particles driven along from the north.

The first night, he camped in the lee of an overhanging bank and built a fire there. He huddled beside it for warmth through most of the night.

At dawn, he saddled up and with considerable difficulty, loaded the frozen body of De Loach. He mounted and, wet and cold, continued on his way.

Snow was still falling, though not as hard as it had the day before. An accumulation of five or six inches lay like a white blanket on the ground.

He dreaded his arrival in town. He knew Tom expected him to bring De Loach in alive, and he knew what the town's reaction would be when they saw De Loach was dead—at least what the reactions of De Loach's confederates in the Little Dry massacre would be. They'd say he'd killed De Loach deliberately because he'd had the chance. They'd say that now that he'd had a taste of blood he'd go on, from one to the other, until they were all dead.

His mouth twisted. He'd never given them any reason to suspect that he was thirsting for revenge. It was their consciences that made them think he was.

He rode steadily and without stopping through most of the day and at last, in late afternoon, reached the outskirts of the town. A boy, walking home from school, saw him first and ran toward the center of town to spread the news.

People came to their doors to watch and people stopped on the street to stare. Johnny kept his glance straight ahead and rode directly to the sheriff's office, where he swung stiffly from his horse and looped the reins around the rail. He kicked the snow from his boots and limped inside.

Tom Ormsby turned to look at him as he came in. "Johnny! God, you look half froze. Come on over by the stove and warm up."

Johnny went over to the stove and spread his hands to its warmth. After several moments he unbuttoned his coat and shoved his hat back on his head. He watched Tom staring out the window at the corpse tied behind his saddle, looking for some critical expression in the sheriff's face. He failed to find it and so he said, trying not to sound defensive, "He put up a fight. I had to kill him."

He shrugged out of his coat. His sleeve was stiff with dried blood from the wound in his upper arm and was stuck to it, but his face showed no sign of pain. He said, "He damn near got me. Pretended his eyes were full of dirt. He got me in the arm and ruined a good pair of boots by shooting off the heel. I didn't have much choice."

Tom shrugged. "He was like all the rest who were in that thing twenty years ago. He figured you'd kill him first decent chance you got."

Johnny said, "And I did. Now they'll all be sure they were right about me."

"They were sure before. This won't change anything."

"I don't know, Tom. If they get scared enough. . . . Scared men do some damn fool things."

Tom said harshly, "Johnny, just sit tight. You haven't done a thing to be ashamed of. If a fugitive puts up a fight . . . well hell, I'd have killed him too, probably sooner than you did. So forget it. Go on over to the hotel and get yourself something to eat. Get Doc to tie up that arm. I'll take care of the body and put your horse away."

Johnny nodded. He watched Tom put on coat and gloves and go outside. He watched him lead the horse away.

He was reluctant to leave the stove, reluctant to go out into the cold again before he was thoroughly warm. But he admitted to himself that he was equally reluctant to face the people of the town.

Not that he was ashamed of what he'd done. Yet he couldn't help thinking that if he had been a little more wary while he was trying to take De Loach, if he had kept his gun on the man, De Loach would have had no opportunity to snatch out and use that revolver. He'd still be alive.

Almost angrily, he grabbed his coat and put it on. He crammed his hat down on his head. He went out and slammed the door behind.

Doc's office was over the bank half a block up the street. He climbed the outside stairs and opened the door at the top. Doc was sitting at his desk, reading a well-worn medical book.

Doc was stocky, short and untidy. He peered at Johnny over the tops of his gold-rimmed spectacles. "Need me for De Loach?"

Johnny shook his head. "He's dead. But you can tie up my arm for me." He shrugged out of his coat. "And you can tell the people of this town that you did. If they know De Loach shot me, maybe they won't blame me so much for killin' him."

Doc went to the rear of the office and got a pan half full of hot water from the stove. He poured cold water into it until it was luke warm. He began to soak the shirt where it was stuck to the wound with a dripping cloth. A muscle in Johnny's jaw tightened.

After several moments Doc tugged the sleeve loose and Johnny took off the shirt and the upper half of his underwear. Doc said, "Sit down."

Johnny did. Doc washed the wound, which was not deep, and put some salve on it. He bandaged it carefully.

"Anything else?"

"No sir. Unless you can fix the bootheel he shot off for me."

Doc peered closely at him, grinning. "Try the shoemaker. How come he got a chance to hit you twice?"

Johnny shrugged expressively. I guess you could call it a miscalculation on my part. He claimed his eyes were full of dirt and I let down my guard. Soon as I did, he yanked his revolver and started blasting away. He'd have got me too if I hadn't got him first."

Doc nodded noncommittally. Johnny said, "Send your bill to the county."

"All right, Johnny. The arm feel better?"

"Uh huh. Thanks."

He went out and down the stairway, which was still slick with snow, walking carefully because of the boot and the ice.

At the bottom he stopped and fumbled for sack tobacco and papers. He made a cigarette, thinking of Gerda. Maybe it would be a good thing all around if he got Tom to let him take off a couple of weeks. Maybe in a couple of weeks people would have forgotten De Loach.

Drawing deeply on the cigarette, he turned left and went into the lobby of the hotel. He hobbled across the white-tiled floor to the dining room, inwardly cursing the missing bootheel.

It was practically deserted. He sat down near the door and when Susan Dahlstrom came to wait on him he said, "A steak, Susan, and about three eggs. While they're cooking, bring me the coffee pot."

She smiled and nodded, but he could see that she had heard the story too. Something was changed in the way she looked at him, something elusive as though she had just seen a streak of wildness in something she thought was tame.

Johnny watched her walk away and anger faintly stirred him. She returned, bringing the coffee pot and a cup. She poured it full and put the pot on the table.

Johnny gulped the scalding stuff. He still hadn't completely gotten rid of his chill, but the coffee helped. He finished the first cup and poured another.

Something must be wrong with him. Maybe he should be as vengeful as the people of the community expected him to be. Maybe he ought to go out and kill the men who had been at Little Dry Creek, one by one.

He shook his head ruefully. It just wasn't in him to feel that way. He hadn't known his parents or any of the other Indians who had been massacred at the Little Dry. All he had known was this town, and Tom Ormsby, and the people with whom he had lived and gone to school.

He remembered that there had been a time when the kids had looked up to him because he was a full-blooded Cheyenne, and he grinned to himself, thinking how pleasant it had been.

But that time had passed, and as he grew older he had begun to run into adult prejudice. He'd tried to get a job often enough during those last years in school, but nobody would give him one. Finally, after the ninth grade, he'd managed to get a job on a ranch fifteen miles from town.

That lasted almost a year. Until one of the other hands, whose parents had been killed by Indians, made his taunts so plain that Johnny could no longer let them pass. There had been a fight, one he remembered clearly yet. When it was over, the other puncher lay unconscious and bleeding on the ground with a broken arm and a broken collar bone. Johnny got fired.

After that, he cleaned up at the Buckhorn, early in the morning before they opened up. He swept and mopped the lobby of the hotel. He broke horses occasionally for Si Deane at the livery barn, and shoveled manure and straw out of the stalls. When he was nineteen, three years ago, Tom put him on as deputy.

From the beginning he'd been extremely proud

CHAPTER 5

TOM GOT THE HORSES and brought them to the office door. The crowd retreated to the far side of the street where they stood, a silent, sullen group watching the jail impassively. The sun was down, but there was still an orange glow on the clouds. Not much light for what they had to do, thought Johnny. Nobody had said how far from town Chavez's body had been found. But it must be fairly close, or Tom wouldn't bother to go out tonight.

Johnny paced nervously back and forth. Uneasiness crawled in his mind. Coincidence, maybe, that Chavez had been killed today. Coincidence, perhaps, that his body had been found less than two hundred yards from Johnny's trail. But he didn't believe it was coincidence and he had a strange, certain feeling that this was not the last of it.

Tom beckoned him and Johnny put on his hat and went outside. He swung to the horse's back and dug his one remaining spur into the animal's ribs. He heard a shout from someone in the crowd as he followed Tom swiftly down the street. He couldn't make out the words but he could make a rough guess what they were.

The pair quickly left the town behind and rode east along the trail Johnny had made coming in.

Light faded from the clouds and the sky turned gray. Light began to fade from the land.

About a mile from town, Tom began casting back and forth, looking for other trails. A quarter mile farther on, he found the inert body of Fidel Chavez lying face down in the snow.

Johnny frowned. What had Chavez been doing here in the first place? Lately he'd been running a band of sheep a dozen miles west of town. He almost never left those sheep.

He swung right and trotted his horse swiftly for about four hundred yards without crossing another trail. Then he began to circle.

Halfway around the circle, he crossed his own trail, went on, and coming back crossed it again. Before he completed the circle he crossed another trail, undoubtedly that of Len Diggs, who had discovered the body, approaching it and then going back toward town.

He rode back to where Tom was sitting his horse looking puzzledly at the ground. He said, frowning with frustrated anger. "Diggs was right. There are no other trails, at least within four hundred yards of the body. It looks pretty cut and dried. Either I killed Chavez or Len Diggs did."

"Why would Diggs kill him? And what the hell was Chavez doing here in the first place?"

Johnny shrugged. He stared down at the trail Chavez's horse had made. The trail had been coming from the west, heading east. Beyond the body the trail continued eastward for about a hundred yards, then stopped, then turned and went, with some aimlessness, back toward town.

Johnny said, "Just a minute."

It was rapidly getting dark and he wouldn't be able to see the trail more than another few minutes at best. He dug his spur into his horse's sides and thundered away along the trail of Fidel Chavez's riderless horse. He followed it for almost a quarter mile at a hard run, then whirled his horse so abruptly that the animal almost fell.

His eyes were intent as he returned, still at a run. He hauled up beside the body. He said, "Take a close look, Tom. Doesn't it strike you that those prints are pretty deep for a horse that ain't being rode?"

Tom dismounted and studied the prints in the fading light. He glanced up. "Maybe. Maybe not. Why?"

"That horse was carryin' double up until the time Chavez was dumped off. He was still being ridden when he went away from here. The tracks are aimless for a little ways, but before they've gone a quarter mile they're lined out straight for town."

He swung from his horse. He stooped and turned Chavez's body on its back. There was a bloody swelling on the left side of the chest and there was blood on the snow where he had lain. But no pool, as there would have been if he had been shot right here.

Johnny said, "Chavez wasn't killed here at all. He was shot somplace else, loaded on a horse, brought here and dumped off. There's hardly any blood on the ground."

"Maybe he bled internally." There was a puzzled frown on the sheriff's face.

"Like hell. Take a look at his shirt and vest. Does that look like the bleeding was inside?"

41

Tom whistled. "Good God, I think you're right. Let's get on the trail of that horse that brought him here. We can pick up the body later on."

Tom swung to his horse and Johnny followed suit. Both men pounded away on the trail of the horse Chavez had been brought on. The light continued to fade and they had gone less than a mile when they were forced to halt. For a long time afterward, Tom sat his horse without moving, without speaking. At last he said, "He was lined out straight for town and he was bein' rode, just like you say. Come on, let's go back and pick Chavez up."

He turned and walked his horse in the direction they had come. Pacing him, Johnny asked, "What do you make of it? Why? . . ."

"Somebody's after you, Johnny. They want you so bad they don't care what they have to do to get you. Chavez was killed and dumped off out there just to throw suspicion on you."

"It worked, too. I'll bet there isn't a man in town that doesn't think I killed Chavez. After the story Len Diggs told."

Tom said thoughtfully, "First De Loach and now Chavez. Two of the men who were in on the massacre at Little Dry Creek twenty years ago. I wonder. . . ."

Johnny said unbelievingly, "You wonder what? Who's going to be next? Good God Almighty, Tom, surely you don't think anybody would go that far? Why don't they just shoot me, if they want me that bad?"

"Maybe they will. Watch yourself."

They reached the body of Chavez. Tom dismounted, saying, "We'll put him on my horse. You and I can ride double going back."

"All right." Johnny lifted Chavez's body to a standing position by putting his hands beneath Chavez's armpits. Stooping, he put his shoulder under the body and lifted it. He walked to Tom's horse and slung the body across the saddle.

As he did so, one of Chavez's hands brushed his face. It was cold as ice. He slid a hand under Chavez's shirt and found that the body was equally cold. He said, "He's stone cold, Tom."

"Figured he would be." Tom tied the body down. He said, "Let's go," and swung to the back of Johnny's horse, holding the reins of the other one.

Johnny swung up behind, reined around and headed back toward town. He still could not believe that this was happening. Nor could he rid himself of the crawling, eerie certainty that it had just begun.

He asked, "What are you going to do? Nobody's going to believe what we tell them about that trail. They'll say you're just trying to cover up for me."

Tom Ormsby's voice was a growl. "Let 'em! I'm not going to charge you and throw you in jail for something I know you didn't do. I don't care if the whole town howls for your blood."

"I've been thinking. Maybe if I took a couple of weeks off. . . ."

"Where would you go?"

"I was thinking I might go over to Collinsville."

"Gerda?"

"Uh huh."

For a time the sheriff was silent. Then he said,

"I think that's a good idea. Meantime I'll look into what's going on around here. Maybe I can turn something up."

They reached town, which at this hour seemed deserted since nearly everybody was inside eating supper. Both men swung down in front of the sheriff's office. Tom said, "You go inside. I'll drop the body off."

Johnny started to protest, then stopped. Tom had a reason for everything he did. His reason this time was that he didn't want Johnny riding down the street towing another body along behind.

He went into the office, struck a match and lighted the lamp. He went out back and got an armload of wood. He brought it in and built up the fire in the stove. When he was sure it was started, he took the bucket and went out back to the pump. He drew a bucket of water, the light from the open doorway illuminating both him and the pump.

For the first time in his life he felt uneasy standing like this in the light. He clenched his jaws against the desire to duck out of it. He finished, took the bucket back in and slammed the door behind.

Why had he felt that way out there? If there had been someone watching him who meant him harm, they'd have shot him and had it over with.

He tried to drive away the growing feeling of uneasiness by scoffing at himself and failed. He was not fool enough to believe that, suddenly after all these years he was developing nerves. He wondered if, perhaps, somebody's conscience hadn't gotten beyond that person's ability to control. Maybe seeing Johnny every day was too strong a reminder of the massacre twenty years ago. But it seemed farfetched that such a thing could be a motive strong enough for murder.

He sat down at the sheriff's roll-top desk, listening to the fire roaring in the flue. He reached for pencil and paper absently. He wrote a name, that of Bradford Gore.

That Gore had been the leader of the massacre there was little doubt. Gore had been the most influential of the men twenty years ago, and was today.

He still owned the same ranch he had then, twenty-five miles to the west of town. The massacre site was on Gore's land. But Gore didn't live there often any more. He spent most of his time at the capital, where he owned a flourishing drygoods store. He'd be spending more and more of his time down there. He wanted to be governor and he might make it, too.

Johnny wrote another name, that of Karl Asbury. Asbury owned the newspaper in town. It was called the Box Elder Post and came out once a week.

Johnny liked Karl; he always had. Karl was a big, bony man in his early fifties, whose deep-set, brooding eyes and gaunt, ugly face were reminiscent of paintings Johnny had seen of President Lincoln.

Johnny shook his head. He wrote the name of Ernst Hunsicker, and now he frowned slightly. Hunsicker owned the livery stable and employed Si Deane to run it for him. He also owned a horse ranch bordering that of Bradford Gore. He spent all his time in town.

Hunsicker was fat and the tightest man with a dollar Johnny had ever known. His horses were always thin and once or twice Tom had threatened to jail him if he didn't feed them more. There was a rumor around town that Ernst also owned a third interest in the bank, but Johnny knew that might not be true. One thing was certain, though. Hunsicker had enough.

Johnny wrote Jake Fahnstock's name under that of Hunsicker. He shook his head almost immediately. Fidel Chavez had gotten heavier through the years. He must have weighed a hundred and seventy pounds. It would take a stronger man than Jake to lift him on a horse.

But his mind dwelt on the man. Jake's luck, for as long as Johnny could remember at least, had all been bad. First he'd lost his wife, and a year later had lost his boy, who had been about Johnny's age, through an accident with a .22. Not long afterward, his fifteen-year-old daughter had run off with a dress-goods drummer and his efforts to trace her had been futile. As though that were not enough, Jake had developed consumption and in the last year or two had shrunk to less than a hundred pounds. He coughed incessantly and most people didn't give him more than a year or two to live.

Johnny heard the door and swung his head. Tom came in, stamping his boots, and closed the door behind. He tossed Johnny a pair of extra boots that he'd brought from home.

Johnny bent over, pulled off his own, and pulled the others on.

Tom coughed and went over to the stove. He

spread his hands to it. "When do you want to go?"

Johnny shrugged. "In the morning I guess."

"Why don't you go tonight?"

Johnny stared at him but he couldn't see Tom's face. "Why?"

Tom swung around. He looked as though he were about to explode. "People! Honest to Christ, the more I see of them the less I think of them!"

Johnny asked, "What are they doing, talking wild?"

"Yeah. I think it might be better if you weren't around here for a week or so. Things will have calmed down some by the time you get back."

"I don't like to run just when things get tough."

He got up and walked to the window. He stared outside. It was completely dark, but there was light coming from the windows of the Buckhorn, and in this light he could see the shapes of men entering it. He said, "The Buckhorn's busy tonight."

Tom didn't reply. Johnny swung around, unbelief in his eyes. "You aren't thinking lynch mob, are you Tom? You don't seriously think? . . ."

"Hell no, I'm not thinking lynch mob. They'd just better not try anything like that!" But he wouldn't meet Johnny's gaze, and Johnny knew he had been considering possible violence on the part of the people of the town.

The whole trouble was, as both of them knew, that Tom had raised Johnny and thought of him as a son. The townspeople didn't expect Tom to be fair and impartial where Johnny was concerned.

Johnny asked, "Did you tell anybody about Chavez?"

Tom shook his head. "You and me know he was hauled out there and dumped. You and me saw the tracks and the ground underneath the body. But how many men in this town can read a trail? And even if I could drag a dozen of 'em out there in the morning, what good would it do?"

Johnny shrugged. "None, I guess." He frowned. "But what if they begin puttin' pressure on? You'll have to arrest me for killing Chavez, and I'll have to go to trial."

Tom's eyes were fierce. "I'll never do it. Nobody can make me arrest you for something I know you didn't do. Thing I've got to do is find the man that really did kill Chavez. And I can work at it a sight easier if you ain't around."

Johnny reached for his hat. "All right. I'll go get a horse. Send word to me if you need me before two weeks are up."

Tom nodded. Johnny went out and closed the door behind him.

CHAPTER 6

HE STOOD for a moment on the boardwalk in front of the sheriff's office. He'd wanted a couple of weeks off to go over to Collinsville. Yet now he could stir up little enthusiasm for it. Nor did he think that being gone two weeks was going to change anything—unless Tom managed to find the real killer of Chavez while he was away.

Tom didn't have much to go on. Just the tracks of a horse heading back toward town. They would probably lead him straight into town where they would be lost in the streets. Tom might backtrack the horse, though. Finding where it had come from might help tell him where Chavez had really been killed.

Unwillingly, Johnny crossed the street to the livery barn. He went in and shouted for Si Deane, the stableman. He got no answer, so went back to the stalls where he selected a fresh horse belonging to Tom. He led him, haltered, to the tackroom where he bridled him and put his saddle on. He led the horse outside, mounted, and rode east toward Collinsville.

He rode about half the distance there before he stopped and camped. He built a fire, wrapped himself in his blanket and went to sleep. The sun woke him, beating directly into his eyes.

He got up, saddled his horse and mounted. At

49

the first stream he dismounted and washed, then remounted and went on.

He wondered what was happening in Box Elder, wondered how Tom had made out backtracking Chavez's horse. Perhaps Tom already had the killer in jail.

The miles fell slowly behind as the sun climbed across the sky. The air warmed and the snow underfoot began to melt. By the time he reached Collinsville, in mid-morning, most of the snow was gone.

He went immediately to the hotel, wanting to clean up and shave before he saw Gerda. He took a room, then went to the kitchen where he got hot water and carried that up too.

He dumped the water into the wooden tub, shed his clothes and climbed in. When he was finished, he dressed and shaved. He put on a clean shirt he always carried stuffed in his saddlebags.

He started for the door, then on an impulse he couldn't explain, crossed the room to the window and looked down into the street.

A dozen riders were entering town, traveling at a hard, fast trot. He recognized a few of them immediately and froze where he stood.

They hauled up in front of the hotel. Ernst Hunsicker, sitting his horse like a sagging lump, yelled, "Couple of you go around the back! Couple more stay here with me! The rest of you go inside an' dig him out!"

There was no doubt at all in Johnny's mind who Hunsicker meant. He meant him.

Nor was there doubt in his mind what they meant to do. They had no intention of hauling him back to Box Elder for trial. Though Tom had refused to admit it the night before, he had been concerned about just this sort of thing. His concern had apparently been caused by talk he had heard in town.

Johnny whirled from the window. They weren't going to get their hands on him if he could help it.

The hall was deserted. He closed his door, locked it and pocketed the key. It would take them time to break it down. Those few minutes might mean the difference between getting away and not getting away.

He raced along the hall to a narrow stairway at the far end of it. He took the stairs three at a time to the third floor.

Immediately above the head of the stairs there was a trap door leading to the roof. Johnny ran along the hall until he found a closet opening onto the hall. He yanked it open.

It was the chambermaid's broom closet. In addition to her cleaning supplies it also contained a stepladder.

He snatched it and carried it back to the stairway. He climbed up, opened the trap door and stuck his head out to look around.

The roof was flat. He climbed out quickly, hooking the ladder with his toe as he did and pulling it after him. He closed the trap door.

He was safe for the moment. They'd search the hotel for him and when they didn't find him they'd assume he'd gotten away. They'd probably search through the rest of the town before anyone thought of looking here. But they'd think of it eventually. And then he'd be trapped.

He eased across the roof, walking carefully so

that the sounds would not carry through to the rooms below. Reaching the edge, he knelt and peered over the wooden parapet.

Hunsicker and two others were still sitting their horses immediately in front of the hotel. One of them had Johnny's horse in tow.

He let his glance wander along the street. He could see Gerda's restaurant and could see her standing in front of it. As he watched, she lifted her skirts and ran across the street to the livery barn.

She disappeared inside. Johnny frowned with puzzlement, but he kept watching the livery stable door. He didn't see her emerge from it, but he did see her come from behind the stable, leading a pair of saddled horses.

She crossed the street and tied both horses in front of the restaurant. Then she disappeared inside.

Johnny stared down at the horses. Both were tall, strong, rangy animals, one a sorrel, the other brown. Neither was the type of horse you usually got when you rented a stable horse.

Gerda was using her head, Johnny thought. She knew he was here. She knew Hunsicker and his men were after him. She didn't care what Johnny was supposed to have done. She was willing to help him get away. She was, apparently, intending to go away with him, else she would have gotten only one horse.

The distance between him and the two saddled horses in front of the restaurant looked like a thousand miles. How in the hell was he going to get down and reach them?

He glanced down again at the street in front of

the hotel. He saw half a dozen men stream from the hotel entrance. Their voices carried clearly up to him.

The voice of Rene Le Gros: "He ain't in there, Ernst. He must've seen us comin' an' got out the back door before Tony an' Jess could cover it."

From the roof, Hunsicker looked like a bulging sack of grain. His voice was hoarse and deep. "All right, then, we'll search the whole goddamn town. I want him, you understand? I want the murderin' redskin and I want him now. Rene . . . Floyd . . . you two take his horse an' cover the livery. See that he doesn't get another horse."

The two rode across the street, one of them trailing Johnny's horse. The others milled in the street for a few minutes as those who had been inside the hotel untied their horses and mounted.

The shot, coming unexpectedly from the extreme northern edge of town, startled Johnny. Then he heard Hunsicker yell, "It's him! Get on up there before he gets away!"

Johnny hesitated only a moment more. Then, suddenly, he understood. He raced back across the roof, yanked open the trap door. He lowered himself through and dropped to the floor. He raced down the stairs, taking them two and three at a time.

His gun was in his hand as he raced across the lobby. The clerk started to reach under the counter, but stopped when Johnny barked, "Don't!" The man put both hands on the counter, palms flat.

Johnny went out the door. If he'd guessed wrong. . . . Well, if he'd guessed wrong he was in trouble. It was as simple as that.

But he hadn't guessed wrong. Gerda was already mounted, heading toward him with the sorrel in tow.

Johnny holstered his gun and ran toward her. He snatched the reins from her and swung astride. He grinned, but was too breathless to speak.

Behind him, as he spurred away, he heard a howl. Immediately following it he heard a volley of shots. He saw dust kick up to the right of him.

He turned his head and yelled, "You stay here! That was too damned close!"

Her horse didn't slacken his pace. She rode leaning slightly forward. Her hair had come unpinned and now whipped out behind her head like golden flame. She shook her head firmly. There was a smile on her mouth, a determined smile, but her eyes were frightened.

He yelled, "Damn it, pull away! You might get hit!"

She turned her face away from him. She didn't slacken her pace or veer aside.

Johnny dropped back. He couldn't make her stop without losing valuable time himself. But he could stay between her horse and the men behind.

They left the town behind, leading their pursuers by less than two hundred yards. The men behind them no longer rode in a group, but were strung out for a hundred yards as the faster horses forged ahead, as the slower ones fell behind.

Shots still racketed behind them, but Johnny didn't worry much about being hit. No one can shoot accurately from a running horse, no matter what the range.

He glanced ahead at Gerda, then at Gerda's horse. He cursed softly under his breath. The brown horse she was riding was lame. Right now it wasn't bad enough to appreciably slow him down, but it would get worse. It ruined their chances of getting clear away.

He briefly considered snatching her off her horse and letting his own carry double, but he knew that wouldn't work either. Double weight would cut down the advantage his own horse had of being fresh.

There was only one solution and while he didn't mention it to her yet, he knew it was something they would eventually have to do. They'd have to separate. He'd have to go on while Gerda fell behind.

Hunsicker and the others weren't after Gerda anyway. They'd let her go. They weren't men who would harm a woman, even for aiding him to escape. She would be in no danger at all.

Her horse stumbled and nearly fell. When he recovered his limping was more pronounced. Gerda's face was white, her eyes wide and scared as she glanced at Johnny.

He swung his head and looked behind. Their lead had decreased to a hundred and fifty yards. He yelled, "You'll have to fall back! We're losing ground! I'll get this straightened out and then I'll come back. All right?"

She nodded reluctantly. He could see she was afraid. He shouted, "They won't hurt you! It's me they want! You go back to town and wait!"

She nodded again. He reached over, took her

hand and squeezed it briefly. She tightened her reins slightly and he forged instantly ahead. He touched spurs to the horse's sides and felt him lunge forward willingly.

He turned his head. Gerda was pulling up. Three of the men leading raced past her and kept coming. The others pulled up, their horses plunging, and encircled the girl.

Johnny frowned. Damn them, if they touched her. . . .

His horse sailed over a dry wash, pounded up a long rise and thundered over its crest. The scene behind was temporarily lost to his view.

Gerda's hands were full for several moments, managing her plunging horse. When she finally brought him to a stop, she was surrounded by angry men. She glanced in the direction Johnny had gone, and saw him disappearing over a rise.

His lead had increased to almost a quarter of a mile. She knew that now, alone, he would get away.

She returned her attention to the men surrounding her. One of them was a great, fat lump of a man with tiny eyes half buried in the folds of flesh surrounding them. His face was covered with an untidy growth of graying whiskers and shone with beads of sweat in spite of the coldness of the day.

This one rode close to her and swung an arm that was like a club. The flat of his huge hand struck the side of her face with a force that set her head ringing.

Her horse reared unexpectedly with fright.

Gerda, unprepared, fell out of the saddle and hit the ground with a thump.

The big man dismounted ponderously. He strode to her and stood over her. His face was twisted with rage, his eyes as cold as winter ice. "Bitch!" he spat at her. "You dirty Injun-lovin' bitch!"

For the first time, real terror filled Gerda's chest. Johnny had been wrong. She wasn't safe with these men. She wasn't safe at all. She tore her glance from the hate-filled eyes of Ernst Hunsicker and looked at the other men.

One of them was licking his lips, his eyes glowing with some indecent kind of joy. One was looking at the ground, as though embarrassed or ashamed. The others were as angry as Hunsicker, though perhaps not as filled with hate.

Gerda got painfully to her feet. She looked steadily into Hunsicker's eyes, her own eyes showing contempt and, surprisingly, no more fear. She said, "He'll get away now. He'll get away from you."

For a second time, the flat of Hunsicker's hand struck her cheek. His face was white. His hands had begun to shake.

Gerda managed, this time, to keep her feet, though she staggered several feet doing it. Hunsicker roared, "Build a fire! I'm going to mark this bitch so that no white man will ever look at her!"

He whirled, shambled to his horse and fumbled in the saddlebags. When he returned he carried a circular branding iron.

The other men had dispersed, and now returned, carrying armloads of dry grass and dry buffalo chips. One of them struck a match and a thin plume of smoke ascended the air. The fire grew rapidly to a healthy blaze. Hunsicker flung the iron into it. Staring at Gerda malevolently, he said hoarsely, "Couple of you get her arms. I'm goin' to mark her where it will do some good!"

CHAPTER 7

Johnny Ormsby had gone a mile beyond the rise before the scene behind again became visible to him. His horse was running easily, and the distance between him and his pursuers steadily increased.

Hipped around in his saddle, he stared back, waiting until he could see Gerda and the men who had surrounded her. When he did, he squinted against the ever widening distance.

They were still halted. There were two riderless horses in the group. One of the figures standing on the ground was unmistakably that of Hunsicker, fat, monstrous. The other was as unmistakably that of Gerda.

As Johnny watched, Hunsicker's arm swung and Gerda staggered sideways from the force of the blow.

Johnny reined his horse violently to the left. His pursuers instantly changed course to cut him off. Johnny put his horse into a dry wash, reversed directions and galloped hard along the floor of the wash for a quarter mile. When he emerged from the wash, he saw that he had outwitted them. They had continued along a course designed to cut him off and had not considered the possibility that he might head back in the direction he had come.

Instantly he pointed his horse directly toward the group, all of whom were now dismounted. They had a fire going and for an instant that fact was puzzling.

Two of them were holding Gerda, though, and this in itself was enough to thoroughly infuriate him. His spurs raked the heaving, lathered sides of his horse unmercifully.

Hunsicker was poking the fire with a stick. He knelt heavily, a stick in each hand. When he straightened, Johnny saw smoke rising from the object he was holding with the sticks.

Johnny's face paled. His eyes were like two live coals.

A quarter mile separated him from the group. Hunsicker approached the struggling form of Gerda like a giant toad.

Johnny cursed virulently. "You son-of-a-bitch! You dirty son-of-a-bitch, if you touch her with that! . . . God damn you, I'll spread-eagle you on the ground and cut your goddamn tongue out!"

Hunsicker was now only fifteen feet from the girl. Johnny opened his mouth to yell. . . .

And then he heard a sound that cut straight through him like a knife. It was Gerda's horror-stricken scream.

No time was left. Johnny yanked his rifle from the boot, jacked a cartridge into it. He flung it to his shoulder.

As yet, none of the group had noticed him. They thought he was gone, thought that by now he was several miles away. He took careful aim on Hunsicker, then realized he did not dare shoot for fear of hitting Gerda. There was neither time to stop nor time to fling himself from his running horse.

He put a bullet into the ground well in front of Hunsicker. The report echoed, flat and wicked, over the land.

Instantly Hunsicker froze. His ponderous head swung.

Johnny was mad with fury. His horse thundered down upon the group before they had time to move or snatch their guns. He flung himself from the horse a dozen feet from Hunsicker and struck the man with a shoulder in the mid-section. The impact was like the butt end of a battering-ram striking a wall.

Hunsicker's breath expelled violently. He was knocked ten feet and hit the ground rolling. Johnny, who still held his rifle in one hand, rolled similarly and came to rest half a dozen feet away.

He was on his feet like a cat. The rifle, held in both hands, swung viciously at Hunsicker's head.

Had it struck as he intended it should, it would have shattered Hunsicker's skull like an egg. But as he swung, a hand caught one of his arms, deflecting the swing, making the rifle butt strike only glancingly against Hunsicker's hard-layered head.

The sound was sickening, even so. Hunsicker slumped, unconscious, flat on the ground on his back. He stared at the sky with eyes that were open but without comprehension or feeling.

Johnny whirled savagely, trying to bring the rifle to bear. But they were on him now, from all sides, swinging guns and fists, and when he was driven to the ground, kicking their boots as well.

One struck his forehead and a spur raked savagely across his cheek. They were like boys, trying to kill a poisonous snake. They stamped and beat him frantically until they were sweating heavily and out of breath.

Johnny felt his senses fade. He heard a screaming and his nostrils picked up the light fragrance that Gerda always wore. She was clawing and pulling and screaming at them trying to make them stop. She kept it up until one of them turned irritably and struck her with his fist. Only half conscious, she staggered back, fell, and lay on the ground weeping hysterically.

Johnny's ribs were one gigantic ache. His head rang with the repeated impact of their boots. His nose was bleeding and one eye was already beginning to swell shut. One of his ears was torn and dripping blood.

It was the end, he realized dimly. It was the finish for him. They'd kick and club him until life was gone. But perhaps in doing so they would satiate their rage. Perhaps they would then let Gerda go.

Not much longer now. . . . But, suddenly, he heard a roar—like the roar of an infuriated bull. Those beating him were flung aside like pins knocked down by a bowling ball. The roaring went on, wordless and yet profane, and there were other sounds, those of a revolver barrel striking human skulls. The beating stopped and there were then only the sounds of Gerda's hysterical weeping and the heavier ones of a man breathing hard with fury and exhaustion.

Johnny rolled over, bringing his hands and knees under him. He fought partway up, to his hands and knees. He stayed this way, head hanging, wondering what had happened and who had interfered.

Pain seemed to encompass every inch of his body. His head reeled with it and objects swam before his eyes.

And then, at last, he heard a voice he recognized. "Johnny! How bad you hurt? The bastards! . . . I got here as quick as I could after I found out the bunch of them were gone. I. . . . My God, if I'd been five minutes later than I was. . . ."

"Gerda. See if she's all right."

Gerda was kneeling beside him, urging him to lie down. He sat up instead, knowing if he laid flat on his back he'd go out like a candle flame. Gerda began to dab at his bleeding face with a cloth of some kind. She had a red welt on her cheekbone, and tear-stained cheeks, but otherwise seemed to be all right.

She was trembling violently, though, and couldn't stop. Johnny put up his hands and drew her head against his chest. He said softly, "You saved my neck back there in town. How did you know? . . ."

"I saw you ride in."

He looked around. The men who had attacked him were beginning to stir and groan, but Hunsicker was still out cold. Johnny said, "Help me up, and let's get the hell away from here."

Gerda took one of his arms, Tom the other. Johnny's face turned gray with the pain. He knew some ribs were broken, but his arms were all right and so were his legs.

Tom asked, "Ribs?"

"I think so."

"Then we'll ride back into Collinsville. We'll get you taped up there and then we'll head for home. I'm not going to let you out of my sight again until this damn thing's settled once and for all."

He and Gerda helped Johnny on his horse. Tom handed Gerda up. Then he picked up Johnny's guns and handed them to him. He led out at a slow walk, without even looking at the men on the ground.

Johnny held onto the saddle horn, his face pale and contorted with pain. Both Gerda and Tom watched his face. Tom rode close to him, ready to catch him if he started to fall.

Johnny was numb, but he kept wondering why Hunsicker and the others had so suddenly decided to take matters into their own hands. The distance back to Collinsville seemed like a thousand miles and seemed to take hours.

They both helped him dismount and helped him into the hotel. He lay down gratefully on a leather-covered couch. Tom yelled at the clerk to bring a sheet to be ripped into strips, and began to unbutton Johnny's shirt. Johnny sat up.

Gerda disappeared as Tom was taping Johnny's ribs. When she came back, she was carrying a small valise. "I got Mrs. Peterson to take care of the restaurant until I get back. I'm going with you. I'm not going to let you out of my sight."

Johnny felt better once the bandages were on. He could breathe again without knives of pain stabbing through his chest. He said, "Let's get on home."

They got their horses and headed west, still traveling slowly because of Johnny's broken ribs.

Johnny stared straight ahead and stoically endured the pain.

The hours passed and the miles dropped slowly behind. They camped that night on the bank of a small stream. Johnny felt hot and feverish and couldn't eat.

It took him a while to go to sleep, for his mind kept pondering the unbelieveability of all that had happened in the past few days. Apparently it had all begun with the death of De Loach. The coincidental murder of Chavez had started it rolling and a combination of fear and guilt had done the rest.

Or was the murder of Chavez coincidental? And if it was, why had his body been hauled out near Johnny's trail?

He fell asleep, but it was not an easy sleep. He kept waking, and once he yelled out something indistinguishable in his sleep.

When morning came, they ate again and continued on toward home. They were very near to it before Johnny asked the question that had been troubling him all along. "What made 'em suddenly decide to ride all the way over to Collinsville after me?"

Tom's voice was gruff. "Because the night you left another of 'em got killed. Floyd Carlin was shot in the back of the head."

Johnny's body suddenly felt cold. Coincidence could be stretched far enough to cover the death of Chavez, and it was not unreasonable to expect the killer to try and throw guilt for the murder on Johnny. But coincidence couldn't cover the murder of Carlin too. Somebody was out to kill every one of those who had participated in the Little

Dry Creek massacre twenty years ago. Or else one of the ten was willing to kill the other nine to get the one he wanted most—the Indian boy who had survived.

CHAPTER 8

JOHNNY HAD LIVED in Box Elder practically all his life. It was the only home he knew and never before, in his entire life, had he known this feeling of dread, returning to it.

His face was pale as the three rode through the scattering of shacks on the outskirts of town. Part of his pallor was caused by pain and weariness but not all of it. His eyes, though virtually expressionless, nevertheless showed a faint wariness he could not conceal.

Unfamiliar feelings were in him today. In the past, he had been able to understand the town's prejudice even though he himself had been its victim. Atrocities committed by the Indian tribes were too recent to be forgotten yet. The wake of warfare always carries its floating debris of hatred that only time can dissipate.

Yet today for the first time, Johnny was feeling resentment. He knew, if no one else did, that he was completely innocent of wrongdoing. He had killed De Loach but only after De Loach had shot him, only in defense of his life.

He knew nothing about Chavez's death, except that it had been carefully contrived so that it would be blamed on him. He hadn't even known Floyd Carlin was dead until Tom told him several minutes before.

And he was hurt because twenty years of exemplary living in Box Elder had been disregarded in a moment of suspicion by people who should have known him better than to believe he could do what they said he had.

Deep uneasiness troubled him, uneasiness that came as close to outright fear as anything in his experience. Something terrible was happening to the town, and it wasn't over yet. Others were going to die, others who had been with the band that attacked the camp on the Little Dry twenty years ago. De Loach's death had given somebody an idea.

There was a scattering of people on the streets. They looked at Johnny sullenly and looked away. They looked at Gerda with open hatred. When the three had passed, they gathered in small groups and muttered angrily among themselves.

Johnny glanced at Tom Ormsby's face. It was hard and still. Tom's eyes were cold, but there was anger in them too.

Johnny grinned at Gerda. He said wryly, "Hail the conquering hero."

She smiled. "They're afraid, Johnny. Don't be too hard on them. Frightened people do frightening things."

He grunted by way of reply, but he continued to study her face. The bruise on her cheekbone stood out darkly in contrast to her flawless skin. Reckless anger touched him. If anyone dared touch Gerda again. . . .

He said, "My two weeks off didn't turn out just the way I planned."

She forced herself to smile. "Trying to wriggle out of proposing to me?"

"Maybe I should."

"Stop it, Johnny. Bitterness doesn't look very good on you."

"Sorry."

Tom, riding in the lead, reached the outside stairway leading to Doc's office over the bank. He dismounted and looped his reins around the rail. He started for Johnny to help him down, but Johnny dismounted stiffly and painfully before he could. He looped his reins, and stared at Doc's weathered shingle hanging at the bottom of the stairs.

The sign looked as though it had been untouched for fifteen years, since Doc first hung it out. The name, Cyrus Greene, was almost unreadable now, and so were the letters, M.D., after it.

Johnny climbed the stairs, stubbornly refusing Tom's and Gerda's help. He went in and they followed him.

The torn ear smarted and his body was one unceasing ache. His face felt battered and swelled. Doc turned from his desk and said, "For God's sake, what happened to you?"

"Horse bucked me off. Get out your needle and thread, Doc. You've got a patching job to do."

"So don't tell me what happened!" Doc said irritably. "Sit down and take off your coat and shirt."

Johnny slipped out of his coat and shirt with Gerda's help. His body was brown and muscular, his shoulders broad, his chest deep. Doc said, "Broken ribs?"

"Uh huh. Tom put these on."

Doc began to unwind the strips of sheet. "Fair job, too." He finished unwinding them and probed carefully with his fingers. He got fresh bandage and began to replace those he had taken off. When he was finished, he doctored Johnny's face with strong-smelling antiseptic and afterward took several stitches in Johnny's ear.

Johnny's face remained expressionless throughout. Doc said irritably, "You damned Injun, don't you even grunt when something hurts?"

"Would it help?"

"I guess not, but everybody does it anyway."

Johnny got up and shrugged into his shirt. Gerda stood in front of him and buttoned it, her eyes very soft and resting on his face. When she had finished she stood on tiptoe and kissed him on the mouth.

Johnny didn't want to go downstairs. He didn't want to face the town. A little muscle on his jaw tightened defiantly. He said, "Let's go, Tom. Let's go see what they'll think up next." He slipped into his coat, which Gerda was holding for him.

He touched her arm and she went to the door. He followed her out and Tom closed the door behind. The three stood on the landing a moment. Then Tom pushed his way through and went down first.

Johnny stared at Tom's broad back as he followed him down the stairs, still holding Gerda's arm. He felt a brief tightening in his throat. He owed Tom a lot. Tom had saved his life when he was two. He'd raised him as though he were his own. He'd given him a name, a proud and respected name.

Now he was standing by with stubborn loyalty though Johnny was aware that some doubt lingered in his mind.

Despite their closeness in all other things, race had always stood between them. It had prevented complete understanding. Johnny wondered why vestiges of his Indian heritage remained in him, particularly since his environment had been so completely white.

Doc had mentioned one Indian trait. He endured pain without any visible sign. And his tracking skill seemed to have grown in him all out of proportion to the training he'd had in it.

What the town really wanted, he supposed, was to chase him out to the reservation. They wouldn't be satisfied until they'd made a blanket Indian out of him. Only they weren't going to get away with it. His heritage might be Indian but he'd been raised white. He wouldn't know what to do with himself if he was thrown into the company of other Cheyennes. He didn't even know how to speak the tongue, with the exception of a few words and phrases he'd learned from Tom.

They reached the foot of the stairs, and from here could see the whole length of the street, both ways.

People were no longer scattered along its entire length. Johnny only saw a few. But a block above the bank, in front of the small, white frame church, there were fifteen or twenty buggies and other rigs. There were a dozen or more saddle horses tied to the picket fence.

As they stood there, people began to file from the doors. They grouped on both sides and after a moment six men carried a casket out. They loaded it into the black, ornate hearse that had been driven up in front.

The crowd dispersed, each to his own conveyance and funeral procession formed behind the hearse as it moved sedately down the street.

Tom muttered, "Carlin. I s'pose I should have gone."

Johnny didn't reply. The hearse drew abreast, then went on by. The mourners began to pass.

Johnny's head lifted. There was an angry, defiant glint in his eye. He muttered, "Damn them, if they expect me to look guilty they've got another think coming." He met each glance challengingly, forcing them, one by one, to look away.

The procession continued down the street. At the very end rode the men who had come on horseback, Carlin's friends from ranches near his. The glances of these were hardest, and there was a lot of muttering.

When the end of the procession was half a block away, Tom went to the horses and untied them. He said, "I'll take these down to the livery barn. Unless you'd rather ride."

Johnny grinned ruefully. "I'd rather walk. I don't want to climb on a horse right now."

Tom mounted his own horse and, leading the others, rode down the street. Gerda took Johnny's arm and walked beside him toward the sheriff's office.

She hugged his arm against her and he could feel her trembling. Looking down, he asked, "Scared?"

"Uh huh. I guess. . . . Johnny, when I saw that man coming toward me with that hot branding iron. . . ." She shuddered. "I'll probably see the look on his face in my dreams."

Johnny remembered his own feelings as he had

ridden desperately toward the group, afraid he could not reach them soon enough. . . .

He forced himself to grin as he looked down at her. He said, "Maybe I shouldn't let you dream alone."

She glanced up at him, a twinkle partially replacing the terror in her eyes. "Why Johnny! What are you suggesting?"

He felt his face flushing uncomfortably. The teasing glint in Gerda's eyes deepened. He growled, "Dammit, don't be so brazen."

"Somebody's got to be. You certainly aren't."

"I might surprise you one of these days."

She looked pleased. "Soon?"

He grunted. "Ahhhhh hell. Behave yourself."

"Yes Johnny." Her voice was meek and he glanced at her suspiciously.

The interchange had lessened the gloominess left in the air by the funeral procession. But it had not dispelled Johnny's dread. Nor had it really lessened Gerda's terror. In the faces of both, as they approached the sheriff's office, was the certainty that, whatever this terrible thing gripping the country was, it had just begun.

CHAPTER 9

SHORT OF THE DOOR to the sheriff's office, Johnny
stopped. He stared at the big front window angrily.

Scrawled there with bar soap, in letters six
inches high, were the words, "We'll get you, Injun!"

He opened the door and let Gerda precede him
through it. He glanced at her face and saw that it
was very pale. He said sourly, "Some damn crank.
It doesn't mean a thing."

Tom came striding across the street carrying
Gerda's valise. He stopped, blocky and solid and
angry, while he stared at the crudely scrawled
threat. He crossed the walk and slammed into the
office. He paced back and forth several moments,
muttering and growling to himself. Johnny
grunted, "Watch your blood pressure, Tom. Don't
let 'em get your goat."

"They haven't got my goat!" Tom's voice was
unnecessarily loud. He grinned ruefully when he
realized it and said, "Well, maybe they have, a
little.'

Johnny asked, "Now what?"

Tom studied him. "You get some sleep. That's
the most important thing right now."

Johnny nodded. "I could use some." He
glanced at Gerda. "I'll walk you up to the hotel."

She started for the door and Johnny followed. Tom said quickly, "You stay here. I'll take her." He picked up her valise.

Gerda glanced at Johnny and then at Tom, her eyes puzzled. Johnny grunted, "All right." He kissed Gerda lightly on the mouth. "See you tomorrow."

"Be careful, Johnny."

"I'll be careful."

The two went out and Tom pulled the door closed behind him. For a moment Johnny stood at the window, staring out at the cheerless street. It was late afternoon. The sky was gray, the sun covered by clouds.

He watched Gerda and Tom walk up the street side by side. He knew why Tom had suggested taking Gerda himself. Tom hadn't missed the expression in people's eyes as they looked at her any more than Johnny had.

Johnny's mouth tightened. The townspeople hated him. They feared and distrusted him. And they hated everyone connected with him. They hated Gerda even more because his race seemed to be of no concern to her.

Tom had realized, if Johnny hadn't, that her association with him was dangerous for her. He guessed he shouldn't have let her return here with him. He should have made her stay in Collinsville.

It was too late to worry about that now, but it wasn't too late to stay away from her until things had been settled, until the town's hysteria had subsided somewhat.

He left the window and crossed to the center of the room. He built a fire up in the stove and stood for a moment in front of its open door, letting the fire's warmth seep into him.

His whole body felt cold. Part of that was the shock of his broken ribs and the beating he had sustained. But part of it was foreboding and dread. Part of it was his certainty that the situation in Box Elder was an avalanche, picking up weight and momentum as it rolled along.

If the trouble stopped now, the town would be quiet again within a week. But if there were more killings. . . .

Wearily he left the stove and crossed to the office couch.

He sat down and pulled off his boots. He lay back and stared at the ceiling above his head. He closed his eyes.

He dozed, and awakened with a start. For a moment, as he dozed he had been reliving the desperate ride back to the branding fire Hunsicker had built. He had seen Gerda, had seen her terrified face. . . . He had seen Hunsicker approaching her, the smoking branding iron in his hands. . . .

He turned his head and stared out the window, frowning. What had happened to the peaceful town he'd known? What had come over it? How could such virulent hatred be born in a short week's time?

He closed his eyes again, unable to hold them open. His body ached. His torn ear, which Doc had sewn up, sent shooting knives of pain all the way through his head.

He didn't like facing the fact, but hatred like that being shown him now hadn't grown from nothing in a week. It must have been there all along, dormant, unsuspected because it had never shown itself before.

The thought was depressing. Maybe they were right, he thought bitterly. Maybe he did belong on the reservation with others of his kind. He was a fool to think he could marry Gerda and live like anybody else.

How much longer his troubled thoughts continued, he couldn't have said. Eventually he dropped off to sleep.

His sleep was no less disturbing than his waking thoughts had been. His dreams were concerned with the pursuit of De Loach and the gunfight that ended in De Loach's death. They were concerned with finding Fidel Chavez's body and with tracking the killer's horse back toward town. They were concerned with Gerda. . . .

Someone not connected with his dreams seemed to be screaming an accompaniment. And this was the thing that woke him up.

The screams were real; they had not been part of the dreams. The street door was open, and there was a woman standing there. . . .

Johnny blinked dazedly. He sat up, swinging his feet over the edge of the cot. He stared.

He recognized the woman immediately. She was Floyd Carlin's widow. He had seen her off and on for years riding up on the seat of the creaking, yellow-wheeled wagon with Floyd whenever he came to town.

". . . you killed him!" she screeched. "You killed him for revenge just like you killed Mr. Chavez and Mr. De Loach!"

Johnny shook his head dumbly. She was dressed from head to foot in black. He supposed she had just come from the cemetery, from burying Floyd. Her hat was askew, her hair mussed beneath it. Her eyes were wild and filled with hatred. Her face was pale, her mouth compressed.

She was almost sixty, he guessed. But she was strong and wiry. And she held a double-barreled shotgun in her hands.

It pointed straight at Johnny, or straight enough so that its load of shot couldn't miss. At this range it would tear a hole in him a man could put a fist through.

He tried to force the remnants of sleep from his mind, to sort this reality from the fantasy of his dreams. Without rising, careful to make no sudden movements, he said, "I didn't kill him, Mrs. Carlin. I haven't seen him for a couple of weeks."

"You're lying! You murderer...."

Her hands were trembling with the weight of the gun, with her fear and hysteria. Johnny knew that at any instant, no matter what he said or didn't say, the gun might go off. Nor was there any defense for him. His own gun, even if he had been willing to use it, was hanging on a nail at the head of the cot, at least five feet away from him.

He said softly, "Mrs. Carlin, I'm telling the truth. I went after De Loach and shot him, but only after he shot at me three times. Tom went out with me to where Chavez was found. We trailed his horse and read the sign. Chavez wasn't even killed out there. He was killed someplace else and dropped off close to my trail so it would look like I'd killed him."

From his sitting position on the edge of the cot, he stared up at her. He could tell she was trying to work herself up to pulling the trigger of the gun.

He found himself wishing that Tom would appear on the street outside. It was the only thing that could possibly save him. He wasn't going to talk Mrs. Carlin out of shooting him. The more he talked, the wilder her eyes became.

He tried anyway. "Tom's been sheriff of this county for fifteen years, Mrs. Carlin. He's enforced the law for all that time and he's not going to stop enforcing it now. If I'm guilty of the things you say I am, Tom will see to it that I go to trial."

Her mouth worked a moment before she said bitterly, "He won't! He won't either! He didn't arrest you for killing Mr. Chavez, or for killing Floyd!"

"But he'll arrest you for killing me."

"Do you think I care? Do you think I have anything to live for now?" Her eyes blurred suddenly with tears. "Floyd is gone. He's lying out there in the cemetery and I'm all alone. Do you think I want to go home to that empty house? I don't care what they do to me."

Johnny sighed. He was wasting his breath, and she had very nearly talked herself up to the pitch necessary for her to shoot.

He said softly, "Maybe you'd better go ahead then, Mrs. Carlin. If you've tried and convicted me, maybe you'd better execute me too. Only what if it turns out later that I didn't kill Floyd? How are you going to feel about it then?"

"You did it all right! You did it! I know you did!"

Johnny's eyes fixed themselves with fascination

on her right hand. It would tighten in a moment. The office would be filled with the roaring of sound, the billowing muzzle smoke. But he wouldn't hear. He wouldn't smell the acrid smoke. He'd be lying here soaking the cot with his blood.

It was now almost dusk outside. Cold air from the open door flowed in past the woman with the gun. With it came the sound of fast pounding hoofs on the frozen street. With it came hoarse shouts. . . .

Johnny forced his eyes to look away from her. He looked past her into the street.

The sound of hoofs was louder now, the shouts more plain. At the edge of Johnny's vision, Ernst Hunsicker, wearing a white bandage underneath his hat, galloped into view, followed by several others.

Hunsicker hauled his horse to a plunging halt in the middle of the street directly before the sheriff's office. Those with him followed suit.

Johnny returned his gaze to Mrs. Carlin, in time to see her turn her head and look outside.

It was the only chance he'd get, he knew. In a moment Hunsicker would come storming in. . . . Or she'd turn back and shoot. . . .

He left the couch in a frantic lunge, pushing with both hands. His feet, wearing only socks, skidded on the floor.

She yanked her head around. She swung the muzzle of the gun. . . .

It belched shot and smoke and sound. Johnny felt something sting him in the side. . . .

He'd never reach her before she shot again. He was only halfway across the room. . . .

But she hadn't counted on the gun's recoil and

she hadn't been braced for it. The gun tore itself out of her hands and she staggered against the wall.

Johnny's body slammed into hers, pinning her to the wall. He recovered instantly. She was old and suddenly terribly confused and afraid. He said, "I'm sorry, Mrs. Carlin. Are you hurt?"

She didn't reply. She stared instead at the shotgun lying at Johnny's feet.

He kicked it and it slid halfway across the room. He said, "Go home, Mrs. Carlin. We'll get the man that killed Floyd."

Her eyes lifted. The hatred in them shocked him. He touched her arm and she shrank away and backed out through the door. He closed it and shot the bolt.

His breath sighed out audibly. He realized that his body was soaked with sweat, that his hands were shaking violently. He stared at the damage done to the office ceiling by the charge of shot. Bits of plaster and dust still sifted to the floor.

He got a cup, went to the stove and filled it with poisonous looking black coffee from the pot. His face twisted, he sipped it thoughtfully, thinking that the hatred infecting this town and the surrounding countryside was like a contagious disease.

CHAPTER 10

Outside in the street, Hunsicker and the others grouped themselves around Floyd Carlin's widow. Hunsicker's arm was around her shoulders sympathetically and seeing that, Johnny's mouth twisted. Last time he had seen Hunsicker the man had been holding a smoking branding iron, approaching another woman as helpless as this one was. . . .

He wondered if Hunsicker could be the killer and shook his head doubtfully. Hunsicker's fury was too violent to be feigned. Besides, Hunsicker's approach to everything was direct. Hunsicker might kill, one by one, the men involved with him in the attack at the Little Dry. But he would be incapable of slyly arranging the deaths so that blame would fall on Johnny.

Mrs. Carlin was weeping bitterly now. Hunsicker sent Roy Beeson up the street with her toward the hotel. Then he turned and faced his men again.

Several of those who had participated in the massacre were among them. Several besides Hunsicker himself. There was Tony Barletta and Jake Fahnstock and Rene Le Gros. With Beeson that made five. De Loach and Carlin and Fidel Chavez were dead. Bradford Gore was down at the Capitol. Karl Asbury was the only one not accounted for.

Johnny shook his head helplessly. Any of the men out there could be guilty of killing Chavez and Carlin. Any one of them.

He could hear Hunsicker's bellowing voice through the closed door. ". . . let's get him out now, while we don't have Ormsby to buck! We can have him strung up by the time Tom gets back!"

Johnny crossed the room and picked up the shotgun. Absently he broke it and punched in a fresh ten gauge shell from the drawer. He put the gun down on the desk and refilled his coffee cup. His hand was shaking slightly, though not enough to spill coffee from the cup.

He doubted if they'd rush the jail. They must know that he'd defend himself, and he didn't think they were ready to risk their lives on Hunsicker's say so. Maybe later they would be, but not quite yet.

He stared through the window at them, a slight frown on his face. He guessed he couldn't blame those who had been at the Little Dry for hating and fearing him. They were frightened men. They had guessed, as Johnny had, that something more than coincidence was behind the unexplained, violent deaths of Carlin and Chavez. Each was wondering if he was going to be next.

But the others . . . the townsmen, the ranchers that made up the bulk of the mob. . . . They had nothing personal to fear. Yet they seemed ready enough to lend themselves to a lynching.

Why? Because they hated Indians, Johnny supposed. For no better reason than that.

He felt himself go loose with relief as he saw

Tom striding toward them down the street. He saw the furious, livid anger in Tom Ormsby's face, and grinned inwardly. His face sobered as Tom drew closer and he crossed the room to the door, snatching up the shotgun as he did. He unbolted it and put his hand on the knob.

Tom would probably disperse that bunch without any help from him. But if any of them showed an inclination to resist. . . .

Tom reached them and stopped, spread-legged, his body thrust forward aggressively. He roared, "Get the hell out of here! Get off the street!"

For an instant, nobody moved though all had turned to face him. Tom bawled, "Move, you sons-of-bitches! Now!"

All of them had guns. Most of them had either rifles or shotguns in their hands. Tom wore a gun but he had made no move toward it. Nor would he, Johnny knew, unless one of them fired at him.

Their glances wavered first. Then their heads went down and they stared at the ground. Then, grumbling, they dispersed.

Tom stood there, angry and unmoving, until all of them had either ridden or led their horses away. Then he turned and came into the office. He slammed the door behind him and went to the stove scowling. He spread his hands over it. He glanced at the plaster on the floor, then up at the hole in the ceiling. He grunted, "I heard that shot but I was upstairs in the hotel."

Johnny said, "It was Carlin's wife."

"Any of the shot hit you?"

"Something stung my side." Johnny pulled out his shirttail and glanced down. He fumbled for a moment in the bandages, then held out a hand to

Tom. In the palm lay two shot. He said, "Bandages stopped them, I guess. But they stung."

He studied Tom's face in the fading light coming through the windows from the dusky street, and he saw something there he had never seen before in his life. Not in Tom Ormsby's face.

It was fear. It showed in the tightness at the corners of Tom's mouth. It showed in his narrowed eyes. It showed in a hand that came, shaking visibly, up to rub his jaw.

Tom swung his head and met Johnny's glance. And suddenly Johnny realized that it was not fear of a personal kind. Rather it was fear that things might get out of hand in spite of all he might be able to do.

Tom said, "I wish to Christ I could figure out what was going on."

"Maybe the answer to that is out at Carlin's place. If we could find out who this killer is. . . ."

"It's the only way we're going to keep the lid on things."

"You don't think Ernst and the others would have tried taking me?"

Tom shook his head. "No. I don't think that. They must've known you'd put up a scrap after the way they manhandled you over at Collinsville, and I doubt if they're ready for a showdown yet. But they will be if anything else happens—if any more of 'em get killed."

"Then maybe we'd better get on out to Carlin's place. Maybe we'd better find this killer before he kills again."

Tom nodded, studying Johnny thoughtfully. "I hate to see you make that ride—the way you feel."

Johnny shrugged.

"But I'm not going to leave you here in town. Not after what happened."

"Then you do think they might've tried something."

Tom said irritably, "Stop putting words in my mouth."

Johnny remained silent. Tom growled, "I'll go get the horses. Not that it'll do any good. It'll be dark before we get out there and I doubt if any tracks are left anyhow. Not with all the people that have been to Carlin's place since he was killed."

Johnny said, "I'll fill a lantern."

Tom nodded, stared at him a moment, then turned and slammed out the door. Johnny got a lantern and began to fill it from the coal-oil can. At least, he thought, the doubt was gone from Tom Ormsby's mind.

He put on his coat and crammed his hat onto his head. He took a rifle from the rack and loaded it.

There were lights up and down the street when Tom returned. Johnny went out, closing the door behind him. He jammed the rifle down into the saddle boot and, holding the lantern, swung stiffly to the saddle.

Tom led out silently, taking the road toward Carlin's place. They left the town behind.

There was a strong wind blowing from the north, a wind that carried the moist, cold smell of snow. Johnny's mouth twisted resignedly. Even the weather was favoring the killer. If it snowed again there wouldn't be a track left anywhere.

Ahead of him, Tom rode hunched and silent.

Johnny thought of Gerda and hoped she would be safe at the hotel. He wondered how all this was going to end. Maybe he'd be smart to take Gerda and leave the country now, before anything else went wrong. If he was gone, Tom could probably find the killer and bring him to trial.

But he hated the thought of running away. He knew if he left now—and there were no more killings—everybody would be sure he was the guilty one. If there were more killings, they'd be sure he had secretly returned.

Besides, Tom really needed him now. Whoever the killer was, he was cold-blooded enough to gun Tom down from ambush if the sheriff started to get too close to him.

Johnny shrugged. He wouldn't run just yet. He'd stay as long as it was possible for him to stay.

The miles dropped behind. They came into sight of Carlin's place as the first flakes of snow began to sting Johnny's face.

Tom dismounted at the gate leading into Carlin's yard. Johnny dismounted too and, using his horse as a shield against the increasing wind, struck a match and lighted the lantern. Carrying it, he walked from one side of the road to the other, studying the ground. There were dozens of different sets of tracks, none of them recognizable in this kind of light.

He glanced at Tom. The sheriff was scowling. Johnny said, "Let's make a circle."

Tom nodded gloomily and Johnny led off afoot. He walked north along Carlin's fence to its corner half a mile from the gate. He didn't see a track.

He turned and retraced his path, and afterward

walked along Carlin's fence to its corner on the south. He stopped here at a wire gate and silently studied the ground for a long time. Looking up, he said, "There have been six different riders through here. Could have been any one of 'em, or none. This isn't doing us a bit of good."

"I was afraid it wouldn't. This is a shortcut to the house." .

"Uh huh. It cuts off a quarter of a mile between the house and town. I've used it myself."

"I don't suppose there's any use going down there to the house."

Johnny asked, "Where was he found?"

"By that haystack right next to the barn. He was shot in the back with a thirty-thirty."

"Long range then."

"Uh huh."

"And no way of knowing which way he was facing when he was shot."

"Afraid not. You know how excited people are when something like that happens."

"Who found him, his wife?"

"No. Dave Nelson. He's been working for Floyd."

Johnny blew out the lantern. He walked silently back along the fence until he reached his horse. Tom plodded along behind. By the time they reached the gate, the air was filled with stinging particles of sleet. Johnny mounted and followed Tom along the road toward town.

In his mind he kept seeing the look of fear that had been in Tom's face back in town earlier tonight.

Something strange and eerie was happening to the countryside. It was almost as though the ghosts of the dead at the Little Dry had come back for their vengeance against the men who had murdered them.

A coldness traveled along Johnny's spine, even though he knew that notion was ridiculous. Ghosts do not shoot guns. Ghosts do not ride horses and drop bodies off where they want them to be found.

No. The killer was real enough. He was someone wtih a reason for wanting the men who had participated in the massacre dead.

But how were they going to find him before it was too late? How were they going to find him at all, when each killing raised the hysteria of those remaining to such a feverish pitch? Johnny shook his head helplessly. The snow drove in heavily on a bitter wind. In minutes the ground was completely white.

CHAPTER 11

Riding through the storm was like riding through a cloud high above the earth. Most times, after the ground turned white, Johnny didn't even see it. All he could see was the swirling cloud of white flakes around him and the dark shape that Tom and his horse made immediately ahead.

He let his head drop forward and closed his eyes. Weariness was catching up with him now. And the pain was constant, the pain of his broken ribs that sent knives shooting through his body with each movement of the horse, the pain of his torn ear, aggravated by cold and snow.

What had happened, so suddenly, to the place he'd thought he'd attained in the community? It was as though it had never existed at all. It was gone, like a puff of smoke. All that was left was bitterness, and the old hatred of whites toward Indians.

He dozed briefly. When he awakened, the snow had diminished to a few fine flakes. The moon, shining from above on the momentarily thinning clouds, put a glow that seemed almost phosphorescent upon the land. No longer did it seem that they were riding in the clouds. Objects—rocks, clumps of brush and an occasional tree—stood out, starkly visible, up to half a mile away.

By landmarks plainly seen, Johnny was able to

place their location in relation to the town. It lay ahead of them, less than a mile away.

Uneasiness increased in him as they approached. Not visible yet, it lay over a long rise of land directly ahead.

He puzzled at that uneasiness. It had been his experience in the past that whenever he felt this way there was cause for it. Had something happened to Gerda? That thought put a kind of quiet panic in his heart.

His inclination was to spur his horse, to hurry on into town. He yielded to it long enough to bring him abreast of Tom. Then, feeling sheepish, he began to drop behind again.

The shots came, flat, wicked and wholly unexpected, shattering the silence of the night in a way that was both violent and sudden. Johnny left his horse in a single, smooth movement, yanking his rifle from the scabbard as he fell.

Rolling in the snow, scrambling toward the cover of some rocks at the side of the road, he glanced around and saw that Tom's horse was as riderless as his own.

"Tom?" His voice sounded unusually loud in the silence. "You all right?"

His only answer was a groan. Instantly he scrambled toward the sound.

The sheriff lay face down in the middle of the snowy road. Panic touched Johnny as he put his hand on Ormsby's shoulder. "Tom! You hit?"

This time there was no sound from Tom. Frantically Johnny groped for Tom's wrist and felt his pulse. It was slow, but strong and regular.

His breath sighed with relief so great it left him weak. Gently he turned Tom over on his back.

Where the sheriff had lain there was a dark stain of blood.

Beneath his chest. . . . Beneath the place his chest had been. . . . Johnny thought, "Oh God, no!" A chest wound was always serious. It could be fatal.

Raging anger briefly touched his mind. He lifted his head and stared furiously in the direction from which the shots had come. He could catch the man. He could pick up his trail and follow it tonight. He could end this business once and for all right now.

But at what terrible cost? If he left the sheriff, Tom would most assuredly be dead when he returned.

Johnny's lips thinned angrily but there was never any doubt in his mind. Catching a killer, even this killer, was unimportant when weighed against Tom Ormsby's life.

He asked, "Can you hear me, Tom?"

"I hear you."

"How bad is it?"

"Bad enough. My whole damn chest is numb."

"It's only a mile to town. If I help you up. . . ."

"All right."

Johnny didn't know whether he was doing right or not. Moving Tom, subjecting him to a mile on horseback might finish him. Yet leaving him could be equally bad.

Besides, a killer was lurking out there someplace. If Johnny left to fetch Doc, the man might finish what he had begun.

He got up and went after the horses, standing

about fifty yards away, their rumps to the driving wind. He led them back.

He helped Tom to his feet, helped him get a foot in the stirrup, then boosted him astride. Tom swayed in the saddle, holding on to the horn with both his hands. He sat doubled up, breathing fast and shallowly.

Johnny reached up and steadied him. After a couple of minutes. Tom raised his head. "I'm all right now," he said hoarsely.

Johnny mounted. Leading Tom's horse close behind him he rode out slowly toward town.

There was no sound in the empty, snowy waste save for the whistling of the wind. There was no movement save for the sifting, drifting snow along the ground.

Johnny hadn't seen the killer, or the killer's horse. He hadn't heard a sound, except for those made by the killer's gun.

Which of them had the man meant to kill, he wondered. Everyone in the country knew that Tom always rode in the lead. Yet the fact that Johnny had spurred his horse just before the shots. . . . The man may have thought that Johnny had forged on ahead instead of dropping back. The bullets might have been meant for him.

Johnny kept looking back at Tom frequently, a worried frown on his face. Tom had been wounded before, but never like this, and Johnny was frankly scared . . . that he wouldn't reach town in time . . . that the wound was too serious for Doc to fix. . . .

He could feel a raw tightness in his throat, a suggestion of burning in his eyes. Tom had picked him up in the village on the Little Dry when he was two. He'd often told him how he'd had to chase him through the village before he got his hands on him. Johnny had been wild as a jackrabbit, he'd said.

And he'd raised him, as though he were his own. Johnny caught himself praying soundlessly.

A father-son relationship is more than a blood tie, he thought. There was no blood tie between Tom Ormsby and himself, but there was closeness. There was understanding. There was affection and respect. Except for the difference in their race, there was everything there ought to be.

He had the feeling Tom was satisfied with him, and that made him feel good right now.

Tom slipped sideways, and Johnny stopped. He dropped back and steadied the sheriff. He asked anxiously, "You all right? It's only a little ways now."

Tom didn't answer him. He slipped farther sideways in his saddle.

Johnny pulled his horse closer to Tom's. He put a leg over Tom's horse behind the saddle and swiftly changed. Riding behind the sheriff, he could steady him with an arm.

It took him an instant to straighten out the reins. Then, leading his own horse and riding Tom's, he continued on into town.

He dismounted at the foot of the doctor's stairs. He yelled, "Doc! Hey Doc! Come on down here quick! I need some help!"

It was several moments before he saw a glow of light upstairs. A few moments later, Doc opened the door and came stiffly down the stairs, clad in slippers, a nightshirt and a coat.

Between them, they eased the sheriff off his

horse. Between them, they helped him up the stairs. They laid him down on Doc's operating table and Johnny raised Tom's legs and began to remove his boots.

Tom Ormsby's face was a ghastly shade of gray. The whole front of his shirt was deep red with blood. His breathing was scarcely visible and he was unconscious.

Johnny's fingers, removing his boots, trembled violently. He kept licking his lips. Through his mind, the phrase, "Oh God, please don't let him die," kept repeating itself again and again.

He had forgotten the town and the murders of the past few days. He had forgotten the man who had fired the shots half an hour before. All that existed for him right now was Tom Ormsby, pale and helpless. And Doc, frowning with concern as his fingers worked with sure rapidity.

CHAPTER 12

WITH TOM ORMSBY'S CHEST BARED, Johnny could
see the wound. It was not a large hole, but it
oozed blood steadily. Johnny felt his stomach begin to jump.

Doc washed the area around the wound, then
got his bullet probes. He glanced at Johnny's face
and said, "For Christ's sake, go sit down someplace. If I need you to hold him I'll call."

Johnny nodded. He stumbled across the office
and sat down in a leather-covered chair. He felt
dizzy, so he dropped his head between his knees.
He stayed that way until the dizziness had
passed.

He forced himself to look at Doc, then at Tom,
so still and helpless on the table. He looked
quickly away. He thought of going back out and
trying to pick up the ambusher's trail, but he
knew it would be no use. By now, drifting snow
would have hidden it.

They were right back where they'd started.
They knew at least one killer was loose but they
had no idea who it was. And you can't fight the
unknown.

Nor would the fact that Tom had been shot
lessen the conviction in the community that
Johnny was responsible for the deaths of Carlin
and Chavez. It would be reasoned that whoever

had shot Tom was probably trying to get Johnny instead. There were plenty of people around who wanted him dead. Hunsicker. The men who had been with Hunsicker at Collinsville. Even Floyd Carlin's widow, though it was doubtful if she could have been the one who fired the shots a while ago.

As a matter of fact, Johnny reasoned, the marksman probably had been after him. There was no reason for anyone to want to kill Tom.

Having admitted this, his mind quickly reached the next logical conclusion. As long as he remained in Box Elder, Tom would be in danger. Gerda would also be in danger, simply because of her association with him.

Bending over Tom, Doc began to sweat. Beads formed on his face. Several times he impatiently wiped his forehead on his upper sleeve.

At last Johnny heard the faint rasping sound of the probe against the bullet. A moment later he heard the bullet drop from the probe into a metal tray.

Doc crossed the room and washed the blood from his hands. He got bandages and alcohol and returned to Tom's still form on the table. Johnny wanted desperately to ask the question that was foremost in his mind, but hesitated a long time because he was afraid of what the answer might be. At last he asked fearfully, "Is he all right, Doc? He'll make it all right, won't he?"

Doc swung his head with nervous irritability. "How the hell do I know?" Then his expression softened and he said, "Sure, Johnny. Sure. He'll make it if everything goes all right. I'll keep him here in the office and look after him myself until he's out of danger."

Johnny nodded. The intensity of relief made him weak. Doc worked steadily, bandaging the wound. At last Johnny asked, "How long? . . . This kind of thing takes a long time to heal, doesn't it?"

Doc grunted, "It sure as hell does. It's going to be a couple of weeks before he can even sit up. It'll be a month before he's on his feet—two or three before he's strong enough to work."

Johnny nodded. "That's what I thought."

Doc swung his head. "And that puts you in one hell of a spot."

Johnny nodded wordlessly. "Somebody's got to hold down the sheriff's office while he's getting well. Only I don't think the town's going to let me hold it down."

Doc asked, "Got any ideas about who's behind Carlin's death?"

Johnny shook his head. He got up and walked to the table. He stared at Tom's face, at his thick, powerful torso. He said, "Want me to help you move him into bed?"

"Uh huh." There were casters on the operating table. Doc pushed it into an adjoining room alongside a bed. Johnny lifted Tom's upper body, Doc his legs. Doc covered him and wheeled the table out of the way.

Johnny asked, "How long you reckon it'll be before he comes to?"

"Morning anyway. You come back in the morning."

"All right." Johnny hesitated, then said

hoarsely, "Thanks doc. Tom means an awful lot to me."

"I know. I like him too."

Johnny went to the door. Doc said, "Good luck."

Johnny grinned faintly. "I'll need a lot of that."

He went outside into the driving wind and snow. There were very few lights along the street, and he saw no one. But he stood at the top of the stairs for several moments, watching the street carefully. Someone had tried to kill him a while ago, and failed. They would probably try again.

He found himself hoping they would. He wanted the man whose bullet had put Tom on his back and so close to death. He wanted that man even more than he wanted the killer of Carlin and Chavez.

Both horses were standing nearby, their rumps to the wind. Johnny mounted his own and, leading Tom's, headed for the livery barn. He put the horses in their stalls, fed them some grain, and walked back up the street toward the hotel. It was late, but Gerda would want to be told what had happened to Tom.

Walking along through the drifting snow, Johnny felt more alone than ever before in his life. Always before Tom had been there if Johnny needed him.

Now Tom wasn't there. Johnny was strictly on his own.

Normally, this wouldn't have bothered him. He'd been Tom's deputy long enough to handle the law enforcement part of the sheriff's job. Sooner or later, he knew, the killer of Chavez and

Carlin would make a mistake. Then Johnny wouldn't be fighting the unknown any more.

It was the attitude of the townspeople and of those living in the surrounding countryside that bothered Johnny. He doubted if they'd let him do the sheriff's job while Tom was recuperating. Judging from the way they'd behaved last night. . . .

He reached the hotel and went inside, accompanied by a swirling gust of snow-laden wind. He closed the door, stamped his boots on the mat, then crossed the lobby to the desk. The clerk was a pale-faced young man named Julius Grout. "What room is Miss Hoffman in?" he asked the sleepy-looking Grout.

Plainly Grout had heard the talk going around the town. He looked at Johnny as though he was wearing war paint. Johnny had a sudden, almost irresistable impulse to utter a shrill war whoop. He resisted it with an inward grin.

Grout said, "Room 14, Mr. Ormsby."

"Thanks." Johnny turned and started toward the stairs.

Grout called, "It's almost midnight. Miss Hoffman's asleep."

Johnny swung his head and stared at Grout with mock fierceness. "I'll wake her up. Any objections?"

"No sir. No, *sir*. You go on up."

Johnny went up the stairs. He was close to exhaustion. The past few days had been rough, beginning with the beating over at Collinsville and ending with Tom getting shot tonight. He hoped that tonight he'd be able to get a few hours of uninterrupted sleep.

He knocked lightly on Gerda's door. He knocked again.

He heard the bed creak inside and a moment later heard her voice just behind the door. "Who is it?"

"Johnny."

The door opened and he went inside. The room was dark except for a small amount of light filtering through the window from the street outside.

He could smell her, fragrant and warm and womanly, and then, as he kicked the door shut behind him, felt her arms go around his neck. "Johnny. Oh Johnny." It was a whisper so soft he could almost believe he had imagined it.

He put his arms around her, feeling the softness, the warmth of her body through the thin flannel nightgown she wore. In spite of his weariness, excitement stirred him. He needed her tonight. And he knew she needed him.

He said, "Go light the lamp. I've got something to tell you."

"No, Johnny. No." She pressed herself closer to him.

He said harshly, "Tom's been shot. Now will you light that lamp?"

She pulled away. She crossed the room swiftly, struck a match and lighted the lamp. When she turned, there were tears in her eyes and her expression was contrite. "I'm sorry, Johnny. I didn't know."

He said, "We went out to Carlin's to look for tracks. On the way back—about a mile outside of town—someone took several shots at us. One of 'em hit Tom in the chest."

"Is he. . . . Johnny, is he? . . ."

"He isn't dead. He's over at Doc's. The bullet is out and Doc says that with any luck he'll make it all right."

She sat down suddenly. Her whole body was trembling violently, as though from cold. She put her hands over her face.

He crossed the room and touched her head. "I knew you'd want to know."

"Is there anything I can do? I could go over to Doc's. . . ."

"Tomorrow, maybe. He's all right for tonight. Doc will have to stay up with him anyway."

"Why would anybody want to shoot Tom?"

He shrugged, and looked away from her searching eyes.

She was silent a moment. Then she said, "They weren't shooting at Tom, were they Johnny? They were shooting at you."

"What makes you say that?"

"Weren't they Johnny?"

"Maybe they were. I don't know. I won't know until I find out who it was."

She got up and slipped into a wrapper but she continued to shiver uncontrollably. She whispered, "I'm scared, Johnny. I'm scared."

He wanted to put his arms around her but knew if he did he wouldn't leave this room tonight. And somehow, staying didn't seem right with Tom so near to death.

Gerda turned her white face toward him. "Take me away, Johnny. Take me far away. They won't let you do Tom's job anyway, and if you stay, they'll kill you."

"I've got to try." He made the statement emphatic, as though it was the only reason for staying. But there was another. Tom had been shot simply because he happened to be riding with Johnny. The same thing could happen to Gerda or to anyone who rode with him. The ambusher wasn't going to quit. He'd try again, and again, until he succeeded or until he was caught.

CHAPTER 13

As JOHNNY went down the stairs to the lobby, he glanced at the clock over the clerk's desk. It was twelve fifteen.

Buttoning his coat, he went out into the wind and drifting snow. He stood for a moment on the hotel veranda, glancing up and down the street. Apparently the Buckhorn was still open, for he could see lights down there, glowing almost phosphorescently through the curtain of snow.

The street was deserted. Johnny walked, head down, toward the sheriff's office. He was beat, and needed sleep, but he kept thinking that, in all probability, the man who had shot Tom Ormsby was there in the Buckhorn, right under his nose.

He reached the sheriff's office and put his hand on the doorknob. Then, yeilding to impulse, he released it and strode purposefully across the street to the saloon.

He opened the door and stepped inside. His coat and hat were covered with a quarter-inch of snow. He stood for a moment just inside the door, batting the snow from his hat, brushing it from his shoulders and arms.

He was almost immediately sorry he had come. Ernst Hunsicker was there, talking loudly to a group of men at the bar. Others who had been at the Little Dry, who had been with the mob Tom had dispersed earlier this evening, were also there.

He should have let well enough alone, he realized. Doing Tom's job was going to be hard enough without flaunting himself at them.

But he was here now, and backing out would be more foolish than staying. He crossed the room to the bar, glancing from one face to another as he did, looking for fear, for guilt, for something that would tell him one of them was the man who had shot Tom.

He saw fear, in one degree or another, in most of them. He saw hatred, blind, dumb and unreasoning. But he saw neither guilt nor panic, and he knew coming here had been in vain.

He reached the bar. He was an Indian and there were laws against selling liquor to Indians. He'd never tasted it in his life and didn't want to. He said, "Give me a cup of coffee, Sam. It's colder than hell outside."

Sam Slagle said, "Johnny, you'd better get out of here. Hunsicker's been talking up trouble all night. Where's Tom?"

"He's up Doc's place with a bullet hole in his chest."

Sam's face showed instant concern. "The hell! Is he ... I mean, will he? ..."

"Doc says he'll live."

"How'd it happen?"

"We were coming home from Carlin's place. Somebody fired several shots at us and one of 'em got Tom."

"And that leaves you. ..."

"To hold down the sheriff's office until he's on his feet."

Hunsicker was silent where he was standing halfway down the bar. Johnny suddenly realized that every voice in the saloon was still, save for his own and Sam's. His words about Tom must have been heard by everyone.

Just as well, he supposed. They'd know sooner or later anyway. Just as well if they understood right now that he meant to stay and do Tom's job until he was well again.

Hunsicker's voice roared out in the sudden silence. "That does it, by God! A damned murderin' heathen runnin' the sheriff's office! He'll get his revenge on us now. He'll get us one by one and claim it's in the line of duty, just like he did with De Loach!"

Johnny turned his head and looked at Hunsicker. He couldn't help the hatred that flooded him because all he could remember when he looked at Hunsicker was the branding iron in Hunsicker's hand and the look on his face as he approached Gerda. He said flatly, "Shut up, Ernst."

Hunsicker's face got red. His eyes narrowed wickedly. He barked, "Ya! You'd like to shut me up, wouldn't you redskin? You'd like for everybody to stand around like dumb cattle while you slaughter 'em one by one."

Johnny said evenly, "One more time, Ernst. Shut up."

"I will not shut up! You murdered De Loach, and Chavez, and Carlin too! Who's next heathen? Me? Me because I talk too much?"

Johnny glanced from Hunsicker's face to those of the others behind him. He had made a bad mistake in coming here. All of them had been drinking and all had been listening to Hunsicker's inflammatory talk. They were dangerous, as dangerous as they had been when they beat him so unmercifully at Collinsville.

Yet he knew he couldn't back away. If he did, if he left here now, his chance of administering the sheriff's office was gone. There was only one thing left for him to do and he'd better do it quickly and well or he'd never walk out of Buckhorn alive,

Hunsicker was about a dozen feet away from him. He turned his head to look at Sam. "Where's that coffee, Sam?"

Hunsicker and the others glanced at Slagle, distracted momentarily. And Johnny moved.

He crossed the distance separating him from Hunsicker in a rush, drawing his gun as he did. He rammed its muzzle into Hunsicker's bulging belly as hard as he could.

Hunsicker released a gigantic grunt. He doubled, his face turning gray with pain. Johnny seized one of his wrists and whirled him, bringing the hand high against his shoulderblades with a vicious wrench. He rammed the gun muzzle against Hunsicker's back. The click of the hammer coming back was loud, clear and unmistakable.

So was Johnny's voice. "Easy now. Easy. Ernst is going to jail but if anybody interferes this gun is just mighty damned likely to go off."

There was some grumbling, but nothing more. Johnny swung his head and looked at the men who had been with Hunsicker. His eyes were blazing angrily.

He said, "Back off."

They backed away uneasily, and Johnny saw

something in their faces that shocked him. It was pure terror. They looked at him the way Grout had at the hotel a while before—as though he had war paint on and a dripping tomahawk in his hand.

This, after twenty years of living among them. This, after going to school with their kids and. . . .

Something twisted his expression briefly. Then he gave Hunsicker's arm an added wrench and said, "Head for the door, Ernst. Don't get any wild ideas."

Hunsicker swung his head and stared at Johnny's face. He looked beyond at the men in the saloon. He yelled, "Don't let him take me out of here or I'll be dead before I reach the jail!"

Johnny said evenly, "You will if you try anything. You can count on that." He yanked the arm an inch higher and Hunsicker grunted with pain. Beads of sweat sprang out of his oily forehead. Johnny pushed him toward the door, digging with the muzzle of his gun.

Nobody got in the way and nobody tried to stop them, though Johnny's back felt itchy until they were outside in the snow. He didn't release Hunsicker's arm, but continued to push him across the street. When they reached the jail he said, "Open the door."

Hunsicker did. Johnny pushed him in and across the dark room. "You know where the cells are. Go into one of them."

Hunsicker opened one of the barred cell doors and stepped inside. Johnny released his arm and gave him a vigorous shove. Hunsicker staggered across the room and Johnny slammed the door. He locked it and withdrew the key.

Holstering his gun, he crossed to the desk and picked up the lamp. He hesitated with it in his hand, crossed to the window and looked outside.

Men had streamed out of the Buckhorn and were now standing in a group before it, staring toward the sheriff's office. Johnny put the lamp down, crossed to the door and closed it. He shot the bolt. No use lighting a lamp and making a target of himself. There might not be many out there that would shoot him through the window but there was one—the one who had shot Tom earlier tonight.

He realized that he was chilled, and remembered that he hadn't gotten that cup of coffee over at the saloon. He crossed to the stove and poured a cup full from the pot.

It was only lukewarm, but he drank it anyway. Then he shook down the stove and built up the fire.

He glanced longingly at the couch but he didn't lie down on it. Instead he walked back to the window and stared outside.

The men were still grouped in front of the Buckhorn, but there were not so many of them now. A few had broken away and were trudging home.

Somewhere in town someone was shouting. Johnny tried to place the location of the shouts without success. He unbolted the door and opened it. He stepped out, listening.

The shouts were coming from uptown. Staring in that direction, Johnny saw a figure running down the street, blurred by the driving sheet of snow.

And he heard enough of the shouts. ". . . it's Jake Fahnstock! He's dead!"

The man turned in beside the bank and raced up Doc's stairs, two at a time. Johnny heard him pounding on the door. Several moments later Doc came out, wearing a buffalo coat and carrying his bag. He disappeared into the snow, hurrying along beside the man.

Johnny frowned. Jake Fahnstock was another who had been at the Little Dry. His death was going to blow the lid clear off everything. Four of the original ten were now dead and only six were left. Even to a fool it was plain that the ten had been marked for death.

Unless this was a ruse—to get Doc away from Tom so someone could slip up there and finish the job they'd started earlier. . . .

Johnny didn't leave the doorway, but neither did he remove his gaze from Doc's outside stairway. If anybody started up those stairs. . . .

The minutes passed. He could hear loud talking over at the Buckhorn, though the wind snatched most of the words away. It whistled against the buildings along the street, and sighed as it drove blinding clouds of snow in through the office door. Hunsicker yelled angrily, "For Christ's sake, shut that door! You want me to freeze?"

Johnny muttered, "I'd rather see you roast," though not loud enough for Ernst to hear.

He wanted to close and lock the door. He wanted to go up there and stand by Doc's office until he came back, then go and investigate Fahnstock's death.

He hesitated for several moments, and at last saw Doc in his buffalo coat coming along the street carrying his bag. Doc went clumping up the stairs.

Johnny whirled and went back into the office. He snatched a shotgun and a handful of shells for it. He picked up his hat and crammed it onto his head. He went out and locked the door, ignoring Hunsicker's yells from the locked cell.

He trudged up the street toward Fahnstock's house. The proportions of what was happening were beginning to be frightening, even to Johnny. He knew that unless he turned up the killer tonight . . . by tomorrow it would be impossible for him to continue as deputy. People would make it impossible.

He passed Doc's office, wondering how Tom was but knowing it would be useless to go up and ask. There was, in all probability, no change in Tom's condition. It was doubtful if he had regained consciousness.

The sounds from the Buckhorn faded from his ears, replaced by the bleak and lonely sound of the wind whistling along the street. Snow was falling thickly again, but it drove along almost horizontally, and drifts were beginning to pile up wherever any obstruction blocked the free sweep of the gale.

As he turned the corner, he glanced back toward the jail, wondering uneasily if the bunch at the Buckhorn would break into it and release Hunsicker while he was gone.

It wouldn't matter particularly if they did, he thought. Hunsicker had committed no crime.

Johnny had proved his point by arresting him and that was all that was necessary.

He continued toward Fahnstock's house, sitting alone at the very edge of town. He seemed lost in a void of swirling snow. It piled up on his coat and hat, and melted on his face and hands, soaking and chilling them.

He thought of the warm stove back at the office. He thought of the office couch longingly. It would be a while before he saw either of them again. . . .

A sudden chill that was not cold ran along his spine. He turned his head toward the sound that had, so suddenly, startled him.

He saw a dim, dark form against the snow. He saw the flare of a muzzle flash. . . .

He lunged forward, diving sideways, floundering on the slippery footing. He heard the flat, sharp bark of a gun, muffled by the snow, diminished by the driving wind.

He heard a wildly shouting voice: ". . . murderin' goddam Injun! You got four of us but that's all you're goin' to get!"

He ducked behind a fence and ran, crouching, to its end. He had recognized that voice. It belonged to Tony Barletta, one of the ten who had been at the Little Dry. He cursed, softly, helplessly, under his breath as he ran along.

CHAPTER 14

HE BROKE CLEAR of the fence and raced across the alley. The gun barked again, flatly, wickedly, and he heard the bullet tear a long gouge out of the fence behind him. He leaped over a pile of tin cans and raced around the corner of a house. He had gone scarcely fifty feet before he heard the tin cans clatter behind him, telling him how close his pursuer was.

No use going to Fahnstock's house now. There'd be nothing he could do. Somehow he had to elude Barletta. . . .

His mouth twisted bitterly as he ran. It was ironic but, frightened of him as they were, they themselves were forcing him to do what they accused him of wanting to do. De Loach had forced him to shoot in self-defense. Now Barletta was doing the same damn thing. If he couldn't elude Barletta, he was going to have to shoot the man. Or be killed himself.

He dodged from side to side as he broke clear of the house and crossed the tree-lined street. Behind him, a dog began to bark fiercely, startled by the shots.

The gun roared again, and again. He reached the protection of another house.

He was growing short of breath and he didn't seem to be having much luck getting away from

Barletta. Trouble was, a man showed up darkly against the white background of snow. Desperation touched his mind.

He ran along the alley and ducked behind a shed. Breathing hard, he waited, the shotgun in his hands. Perhaps Barletta would run past. Perhaps then Johnny could backtrack and lose him in the storm.

He stopped his breathing as Barletta ran into sight less than a dozen feet away. The man was panting hoarsely. He had a gun in his hand and was reloading it.

He went on for several yards, then stopped. He stared at the ground, covered now by four inches of snow and completely devoid of tracks. He turned around. . . .

He saw Johnny standing against the wall of the shed. Johnny barked, "Drop it, Tony, or I'll cut you in two!"

It was like the business with De Loach all over again. Tony was so sure Johnny intended killing him. . . .

He fired almost instantly. The bullet tore into the shed not six inches from where Johnny stood. Johnny tightened a finger on the trigger of the shotgun. . . .

But he didn't fire. He waited, in those fleeting seconds praying that Barletta would change his mind.

Tony fired again, and this bullet ticked through the sleeve of Johnny's coat.

He had no choice now. Tony was no longer startled and wouldn't miss again. With his face grim, with his teeth clenched, he fired and saw

Barletta driven savagely back across the alley by the terrible force of the blast.

The snow was almost instantly drenched with Barletta's blood. Johnny fumbled in his pocket and reloaded the shotgun absently.

Nausea flooded him. He thought he was going to be sick. He took several steps forward and stared at the blood-drenched body in the snow.

It had been so useless, so unnecessary. Barletta needn't have died. But he was dead, by Johnny's hand, and there was no longer the slightest chance that Johnny could do the sheriff's job. Or even stay in town.

They'd be on him, shortly, like a pack of dogs, drawn by the sound of Barletta's shots, by that last, booming sound Johnny's shotgun had made. Shivering, he turned and hurried along the alley. There was nothing left for him to do in town. He could only run.

He hurried down the alley, crossed through a yard and reached the street. Behind him, he heard shouts as they found Barletta's body. He was too far away to distinguish words but there was no mistaking the fury and outrage in the shouts.

He was fair game, now, for anyone. He'd be shot on sight. And he was leaving tracks that a child could follow easily.

Somehow he had to reach the livery stable ahead of them. He had to get a horse, and provisions, and blankets if he could.

He crossed through another yard. Lamps were being lighted in many of the houses now. In half an hour the whole town would be awake.

He crossed through another yard, ran along still

another alley, ducked through a vacant lot and across to another. He was immediately behind the bank now, and could see Doc's lighted windows overhead. He paused for breath beneath the outside stairway, reached down and made a snowball which he threw at Doc's door overhead.

It thumped solidly on the door. After several moments Doc opened it, saying irritably when he saw no one, "What the hell's going on?"

Johnny called, "Doc? It's me, Johnny."

"What do you want?"

"Throw down some blankets, will you? I've got to get out of town."

"Why? Jake Fahnstock died of a stroke."

Johnny suddenly felt limp. He wished Barletta could have heard that before he started gunning through the town for him. He said, "It isn't Fahnstock they're after me for. I shot Tony Barletta a few minutes ago."

Doc said, "Holy Jesus!"

"Yeah. How's Tom?"

"Don't you worry about Tom. He's got a better chance than you have now. I'll get you some blankets."

He disappeared and a moment later reappeared with an armload of blankets. He threw them down and Johnny caught them.

He could hear his pursuers coming. They sounded as though they were less than a block away. He said, "So long, Doc."

"Good luck."

Johnny ducked back to the alley, carrying the blankets, and ran along it until he reached the street. He stopped, glanced both ways, then, seeing no one, ran toward the livery barn.

He entered the stable by the rear door, quietly. He laid down the blankets, went to one of the stalls and bridled a horse. He led the animal toward the front, got a saddle out of the tack room, put it on and cinched it down. He opened the big front door.

Leaving the horse, he returned to the rear of the stable for the blankets, rolling them up as he came back. He tied them on behind the saddle.

Glancing out the door, he saw a group of about thirty men crossing the street, following his trail. They'd be at the rear of the stable in a minute or so.

He mounted and rode out as soon as they disappeared. He'd have to go without provisions. But maybe he could stop at a ranch house someplace where they hadn't heard any recent news from town. . . ."

A block from the livery barn, he spurred the horse. A few moments later he left the town behind.

His face was set in an angry, bitter mold. He hadn't handled things very well since Tom had been shot. But he couldn't see how he could have done much differently. It wasn't his fault Jake Fahnstock had picked tonight to have a stroke. Nor could he have foreseen Tony Barletta's panic at the news.

Running away wasn't going to solve anything. Except perhaps that it was the only way he could stay alive. He couldn't investigate the murders running all over the countryside, pursued by a blood-hungry mob. And if there were more killings, they'd still be blamed on him. It would be said that he'd sneaked back into town. . . .

The snow continued, driven along horizontally on the wind. Johnny knew if he had a fifteen minute start they'd never find his trail. It was drifting over a quarter-mile behind his horse.

After all the shouting and shooting in town, it was quiet riding across the plain. There was only the sound of the bitter wind.

He turned west immediately, and headed for the mountains. He'd have a better chance of eluding capture there than on the open plain.

He shivered, and wished he had a warmer coat. Yet he knew not all of his shivering was caused by cold. His mind kept seeing Barletta lying in the alley, drenched with his own blood. He kept going over that incident, wondering how he could have avoided shooting the man.

He couldn't have avoided it, he concluded finally. Barletta had been intent on killing him, believing him to be responsible for Jake Fahnstock's death. He'd tried to elude the man. When he'd finally faced Barletta, Tony had refused to listen to him.

Now, five of the original ten were dead. Remaining were Hunsicker, Asbury, Beeson, Le Gros and Gore. And one of them was a murderer.

It had to be Hunsicker, thought Johnny. It had to be. It couldn't be Asbury or Gore. Nor could it be Beeson or Le Gros.

He rode steadily through the rest of the night, straight west all the time. Toward morning, as gray began to lighten the horizon in the east, the snow stopped, though the wind continued unabated, stirring up ground blizzards as blinding as the snow had been.

He reached the first of the foothills lying east of

the mountains, rode through them for half an hour, then cut through the hogback where Fountain Creek tumbled through the gorge it had made ten thousand years before. He did not stay with the creek but instead climbed the first of the low mountains immediately across from the rock-spined hogback.

The air cleared as he climbed, as it was freed of the drifting show. Here and there the ground was bare where the wind had scoured it clean.

Halfway up the slope, Johnny stopped to rest his horse. He dismounted, stamped his feet to warm them and slapped his hands against his thighs. He stared back in the direction he had come.

He could see nothing down there, nothing but the cottony blanket of drifting snow hovering close to the ground. Here and there he could see the rounded top of one of the foothills standing above the cloud of drifting snow.

On one of these rounded knobs, his eye briefly caught a moving blob of black. . . .

He hadn't had his fifteen minute start. They'd found his trail and followed it before the wind could drift it in and hide it from them forever.

Undismayed, he mounted his horse and continued up the rocky slope. It didn't matter much. He could find ways of hiding his trail from them.

It wasn't the immediate future that troubled him anyway. For now, he could elude them and stay alive.

But he couldn't stay out here forever. Eluding pursuit wouldn't solve anything, nor would it turn up the murderer.

Thoughtfully, he crested the ridge, stared for a

moment at the land ahead of him, then chose a course and followed it.

He had a lead of several miles. He had time to hide his trail and hide it well. But he wished he had some food. He was going to get damned hungry before they gave up and stopped hunting him.

CHAPTER 15

DEEPER AND DEEPER into the mountains he went as the day progressed, clinging to high ridges where the rocky ground was bare, and sometimes riding for a mile or more in the roily, rumbling water of some mountain stream. Though he caught no further glimpse of those pursuing him, he knew they had not given up. They had simply fallen farther and farther behind.

He wished it would snow again, but there didn't seem to be much chance of it. The sky was virtually cloudless and while the sun shone brightly down, it was without much warmth.

He came unexpectedly upon a deer twice during the morning, and each time snatched automatically for his gun. But he didn't shoot either time, knowing the shot would draw them to him and shorten his lead.

Noon came, and passed, and still he rode. In mid-afternoon he came upon an abandoned cabin, entered it and ransacked it for food. He found a can of coffee, a can of sugar, and a can of beans. Everything else had either been destroyed or eaten by the mice and rats.

He ate a few mouthfuls of sugar, drank some water and went on. He was playing for time now, knowing that when nightfall came he could put ten or fifteen miles between his pursuers and himself. They had been able to trail in the deep snow of the plain all through the previous night, but they couldn't trail up here. Not when his trail disappeared periodically on bare ground or in some stream.

The sun sank slowly in the west. At this time of year, dusk came quickly and early, and by six o'clock it was completely dark.

Johnny stopped in a deep canyon at first complete dark and cleared the snow from a thick patch of grass for his horse. Then he built a small fire and boiled coffee and cooked beans in pans he'd salvaged from the abandoned shack.

He drank the coffee and ate the beans before they were completely cooked. He washed his gear, put it away and went on.

It was a long and endless night. A night of dozing sometimes in the saddle. A night of alertness at other times when he covered ground on which it was possible to hide his trail. At last, as the sun poked its face above the eastern horizon, he reached a peak that was above timber line and from which all the snow had been scoured clean.

He rode the crumbled granite for a good hour, and at last reached a pile of rocks that would shelter him. He dismounted, tied his horse, wrapped himself in the blankets Doc had given him, and went to sleep. He slept a good four hours before he awoke.

They'd find him eventually. But he'd see them from here while they were still a mile away. Then he could begin again the deadly game of hide and seek. For as many days and nights as his horse held out. For as long as he himself held out, although he had a notion they'd give up before they wore him out.

He ate some of the cold beans he had partially cooked the night before. He drank water from a spring. Still tired and very sore, he sat down and stared along the trail he had made coming here.

In mid-afternoon he saw the first of them toiling along up the bare granite slope. He fired half a dozen shots at them, changing the elevation angle of his revolver barrel each time he shot. The last bullet struck close enough to make them dismount and duck for cover.

Grinning faintly, he untied his horse, mounted and rode away through the jagged rocks, using the land itself to hide his retreat.

They'd stay pinned down for a while, he guessed. Long enough for him to circle and get behind them and head for lower country where he could find feed for his horse.

He lifted the horse to a trot on the far slope of the peak, dropped through a thick patch of timber, crossed another bare expanse of granite, and at last reached a narrow, grassy valley at its foot. Here he allowed his horse to graze for about fifteen minutes after kicking aside the snow that covered the thick grass.

Fearing to wait longer, he mounted again and continued down the canyon.

The first indication that they had split up came as a bullet tore rock dust from a boulder less than twenty feet away from him. Immediately afterward he heard a report, echoing back and forth between the sheer canyon walls. And right after that the second shot came, from the opposite canyon slope.

He kicked his horse into a reckless gallop until he reached a patch of timber. Here he stopped, and turned, and studied the canyon slopes.

Three men were on the slope from which the first shot had come. Two were on the other slope. There had been twenty or thirty men in the group pursuing him.

Instead of pinning them down on that bare granite slope back there, he'd only scattered them. He'd given away the fact that he had no rifle, only a revolver with which to defend himself.

That hadn't been very smart, he realized. Now they were spread out all over the place, and the shots fired a few moments ago would pinpoint his location and tell them that he had headed for lower ground.

So instead of contending with a single unwieldy group, he now had to contend with a dozen fast traveling groups, any of which could cut his trail at any time or simply blunder into him as those two groups back there had done.

His horse stumbled on a rotted log and nearly fell. Johnny frowned worriedly. The horse, soft from stable feed, was getting tired. He was tired himself, from poor food, lack of sleep, the wounds and beating he had sustained. He wasn't thinking as clearly as he usually did.

He could hold out today, and tonight, and perhaps tomorrow. But after that he was going to have to change his plans. He was going to have to hole up someplace or he was going to have to start fighting back.

The first alternative was virtually impossible, since he had no food. The second was equally unpalatable because fighting back would simply prove they had been right about him all along.

He wondered worriedly how Tom Ormsby was doing now. He knew it was possible, even likely that complications had developed. They usually did with someone shot in the chest. Lots of men got pneumonia and never recovered at all. Or infection set in and the result was the same.

Doc was good. He'd do everything he could for Tom. And probably by now Gerda was relieving him and taking care of Tom.

Anger touched Johnny at his helplessness. Here he was, running from a dozen groups of kill-crazy men, any one of which would cut him down without warning if they got the chance. And while he was running from them a killer was loose someplace, the man who had killed Carlin and Chavez. A second potential killer was also loose, the man who had shot Tom.

Where it would end, he couldn't guess. There was no law in Box Elder now. Even if Tom was up to appointing another deputy, Johnny doubted if there was a man in town who would take the job. So it would be mob rule until Johnny was caught. It would be mob rule until all of the original ten who had been at the Little Dry were dead. Or until the killer himself was dead.

The sun sank behind the peaks. The clouds flamed. Twice he saw small groups of men behind him, silhouetted against the sky. Once he saw two men a mile or so to his right.

A flurry of shots ahead of him startled him at dusk. He was riding in thick timber, and immediately dismounted and tied his horse. He went ahead cautiously on foot.

The shots had been less than a quarter-mile away, probably in this same patch of timber. He was aware that the sound of them would draw every man within hearing to the spot.

He risked approaching because of a certainty that, if the shots meant what he thought they did, he now had a chance to catch the killer he was looking for.

Hurrying, but silently, he covered the ground in the time it took for the light to fade. And at last, dark against the snow, he saw what he had expected to see.

A horse was standing, riderless, in a small clearing. Nearby a man was lying in the snow.

Johnny edged through the timber, cursing softly under his breath. Whoever had shot that man down there had left tracks in the snow, tracks that could be followed easily. Except that Johnny couldn't follow them. Not now at least.

He reached the body and instantly recognized Rene Le Gros. The man had been shot in the back.

A cracking in the timber made him back quickly and silently away. A couple of men rode into sight.

They spotted the horse and rode to it. Johnny made his way swiftly back to his own mount.

The search would be intensified now, because not one of them would doubt that Johnny had killed Le Gros. Rene had been present at the Little Dry. He was one of the ten.

Johnny mounted. He could hear others coming through the timber toward the spot, could hear them shouting back and forth. He eased his horse uphill, hoping he'd be lucky enough not to run into any of them.

Once he stopped, and froze, holding his hand over his horse's nostrils, while three men rode past not fifty yards away. He went on afterward, and, when he reached the top of the ridge, put his horse into a steady trot.

A silly ditty the kids used to sing at school kept running through his mind. "Ten little Indian boys." It fitted the present situation with almost frightening exactness. The only difference was that the ten were not Indians, but whites.

They were being steadily whittled down, however, just as in the song. Six of the original ten were dead, two by Johnny's hand, one from natural causes, and three at the hands of the unknown murderer.

Only four of them were left. Asbury, Beeson, Hunsicker and Gore.

Gore was at the Capitol. Asbury, Johnny felt sure, was still in Box Elder. Which left Beeson and Hunsicker.

Of the two, Johnny would pick Hunsicker as the killer any time. Yet if he was the killer, why had he been so infuriated when Johnny escaped at Collinsville? The killer would want Johnny free, to be blamed for his killings when they occurred.

And if Hunsicker was the one, what could his motives be? Why did he want the other nine men dead? If his motive was hatred of Johnny, then he was taking a roundabout, complicated way to satisfy it. And a dangerous way.

Johnny's thoughts reached the same impasse

they always did. Hunsicker wasn't the killer. He couldn't be. It just didn't make any sense.

The only other explanation of Le Gros's death was that it had been an accident. Someone had mistaken him for Johnny and had shot at him. Discovering their mistake, they had panicked and run away.

Scowling savagely, Johnny stopped his horse. One way or another, he had to find out who the men were who were hunting him. Knowing that, it was possible that he could save a life or two. Perhaps he could stop the killings before all of the original ten were dead. And clear himself by doing so.

If Le Gros's death had not been an accident, and he doubted if it had, then the killer was certainly among the group pursuing him.

With sudden decision, he drew his gun and fired it several times. If he was going to find out who his pursuers were, he first must get them together in a single group. They'd gathered back there where Le Gros was killed. More shots, now, would bring them together here.

It was risky, admittedly. And there was no guarantee of success. It was still too dark to see.

He climbed the slope to his right for about a quarter-mile. He dismounted, tied his horse in the timber, and walked to a spot from which he could see the snow-covered valley below. Shivering, he waited for the first of them to arrive.

CHAPTER 16

WAITING, JOHNNY REALIZED how close he was to the limit of his endurance. He could scarcely hold his eyes open. His mind felt drugged, his arms and legs as heavy as lead. His whole body was cold, all the way to the marrow of his bones.

He thought what it would be like to sit down in Gerda's restaurant to a sizzling steak, steaming coffee and hot apple pie. He thought what it would be like to hold Gerda in his arms.

Right now, even a fire would feel wonderful, he thought, and scowled because he knew it would be a long time before he could have any of those enticing things.

He waited almost an hour, growing colder because he stood so motionless. At last he heard the first of them crunching through the snow in the valley below. He could see them dimly against the white background, only as darker shapes, and counted five.

The five stopped a few hundred yards beyond the place where Johnny had fired the shots. He could hear them talking among themselves and heard one man say explosively, "Jesus Christ, it's cold. How long's it going to be before we can build a fire and warm up?"

There was some indistinguishable talk among them afterward, and then Johnny heard one of them say, ". . . wait here until the others come along. Maybe we can camp for the night and pick up his trail tomorrow."

Johnny grinned humorlessly. They were almost as tired as he, almost as cold and miserable. The excitement had gone out of the chase and they all were discouraged. Another night out here in the snow, another day of pursuing him fruitlessly, and they'd all be more than ready to quit and go home.

Another group arrived, and, after a while, a third. They dismounted and began to gather firewood.

Johnny shivered in silence on the side of the hill. The wind was blowing down the canyon, so he didn't worry about his horse smelling those down below and giving his presence away. The only real danger was that one of the groups would blunder into him. That was unlikely, however. So far they had all been riding on the canyon floor.

More groups had arrived by the time the first ones got the fire going well. They gathered around it, feeding it until it was a roaring blaze, until they were forced to back away from its increasing heat.

Johnny counted them. There were twenty-two in all. The body of Rene Le Gros was still on his horse where they had loaded him earlier. He made twenty-three.

Johnny had never made an accurate count of those following him. He had guessed thirty but knew he could have been off by quite a bit. He waited another twenty minutes, however, and was rewarded by the arrival of a group of five.

Judging that this was all, he began to move cautiously down the slope. He stopped while still a hundred yards away. He could distinguish their words now, and could recognize all of them. Of the ten who had been at the Little Dry, only Hunsicker and Beeson were here. But. . . .

He stared unbelievingly. The figure of Bradford Gore was unmistakable, hulking, ponderous, arrogant. . . .

It could have been any one of the three, he thought, who had killed Rene Le Gros. So far as he knew, all had had the opportunity.

The presence of Gore troubled him. He'd supposed Gore was in the Capitol, taking care of his business there and preparing for the election. Johnny shrugged lightly. Perhaps he'd come home to his ranch for a week or so. Perhaps he'd joined the hunters simply because he'd happened onto them.

Johnny retreated up the slope. He reached his horse, untied him and continued over the top where a saddle separated two tall peaks. He dropped down on the other side into another canyon much like the one he had left a few minutes before.

He began to gather firewood. All the hunters were back there by their fire and they'd stay by it throughout the night. He was willing to bet his life on that.

No use freezing himself. No use going hungry when he still had coffee and sugar and dry beans in a sack behind his saddle.

He started his fire and crouched over it, soaking up its heat. When he had warmed himself, he got the grub from behind his saddle and put on a pan of water and another of beans. When the water boiled he added coffee.

He drank three cups and finished up the beans. He tossed the empty bean pan into the brush and restored the other to the sack. He got his blankets and, after clearing a spot of snow, laid down in them.

He slept instantly, deeply, and did not awaken until dawn was graying the eastern sky. He got up immediately. They could have ridden down on him in a body during the night and wouldn't even have awakened him. Grinning ruefully, he tied his blankets on and mounted up. He retraced his path of the night before until he could look down into the valley where the hunters had been camped.

A thin plume of smoke arose from their fire which was now only a dying bed of coals. The ground was trampled where they had been. But they were gone.

They had left a wide, easily followed trail. Johnny rode down into the canyon and followed it. They'd been closer to giving up than even he had guessed. For now, at least, he was safe from them.

The trail continued straight down the canyon. When it reached a larger, wider canyon, it turned down this one toward the east. In the late afternoon Johnny reached the hogback and from its top, saw them far out on the rolling plain, heading for Box Elder thirty miles away.

Wondering why he did it, Johnny continued to slavishly follow trail. And puzzled at it while he rode. There was no further need for following. He knew they were returning to town.

But he stayed on the trail anyway, his eyes casting watchfully back and forth.

Little Dry Creek wasn't far from here. The site of the massacre wasn't over half a dozen miles from where Johnny was right now. He was riding across land belonging to Bradford Gore.

He frowned lightly to himself, thinking of Gore. Gore could be the killer as easily as Hunsicker, he thought, but the theory didn't make much sense. Gore was a big man nowadays, with a bright future in politics. Why should he risk all that just to get rid of the last Indian who had been in the camp on the Little Dry?

The sun sank out of sight behind the mountains, and gray, chill dusk crept across the plain. At last Johnny spotted a set of tracks leaving the others and angling away....

They headed for Gore's place, lying to the south. Gore was going home.

On impulse, he turned into the solitary trail. It headed straight for the massacre site on the Little Dry, which was also along the straight route to Gore's ranch house.

The light faded swiftly from the sky. Before Johnny had gone three miles, the sky was altogether dark.

Snow had thawed on the plain while Johnny had been in the mountains. There was still sizeable patches of it laying around, but not enough to make trailing possible in the dark.

He made camp at the massacre site, a bit puzzled at himself for doing so. He built a fire in a hollow, where it could not be seen from the surrounding plain.

He satisfied himself with coffee tonight, loaded

liberally with sugar to help his feeling of emptiness. Afterward, he left the fire and wandered along the east bank of the Little Dry.

He had been here once or twice purely out of curiosity. He had a collection of arrowheads he'd picked up here. Now he stood and stared at the empty, snowy ground and it was almost as if the tipis stood here once more, as if the fires winked against the black night sky.

His father and mother had died here, and for a little while he wondered about them, wondered who they had been, how old or how young. Had his father been a warrior, or a chief, or a medicine man? Had his mother been beautiful? Had he any brothers or sisters?

All the answers had been in this place once but they were here no more. It was an empty, forgotten spot, that lived only in the minds of the men who had come here to kill twenty years before. And in Johnny's mind.

But the faceless, voiceless men and women who had been murdered were crying out for vengeance after twenty years. They were reaching from the grave for their killers one by one. . . .

That thought made an eerie chill run along Johnny's spine. It was ridiculous, of course. He knew it was impossible. But he walked back to his fire anyway and squatted beside it, waiting for its warmth to chase away the chill.

He stared into the flames bleakly, wondering what the future could possibly hold for him. After all that had happened . . . after all the bitterness and violence. . . . Perhaps it would be better if he sought out his own kind and lived with them. Perhaps the whites would never wholly accept him and maybe the Cheyennes would.

It would mean giving up Gerda—and Tom. It would mean giving up everything he valued: his deputy's job and with it the place he had earned in the community.

He shook his head angrily. To hell with them. They weren't going to force him back into a tipi just because his skin was dark and his heritage Cheyenne. The Indians weren't a proud race anymore. They lived in dirty canvas tipis now, and ate scrawny beef that the Indian Bureau gave them. They drank cheap whisky sold to them by unscrupulous traders to forget their memories of the free, proud days when they owned this land and roamed proudly from one end of it to the other.

Yet unless he could come up wtih the killer of Chavez and Carlin and Le Gros, he didn't dare go back to Box Elder. He wouldn't get halfway to the sheriff's office before somebody cut him down.

The fire died to a glowing bed of coals. Johnny wrapped himself in his blankets and laid down to sleep.

For a long time he stayed awake, staring up at the stars, wondering that his course must be. Somewhere there had to be a place for him, a place to which he could take Gerda and live out his life as he wanted to. All he had to do was find that place.

He slept at last, but wakefully and uneasily, as though the ghosts in this place were haunting him. He dreamed, not of white men's things but of a village here, and of himself dressed as an Indian brave. He dreamed of riding away on a raid against Gore's ranch. He dreamed of getting Gore squarely in his sights.

He awoke, sweating, and got up immediately. He built up the fire and made more coffee, which he gulped nervously. He sat motionless beside his fire until dawn lightened the sky enough to trail.

Mounting, he set out along Gore's trail. For a while he puzzled at his tenacious curiosity about Gore's trail. Did he suspect that Gore was the killer he was hunting for? Or did he hate the man so for leading the expedition twenty years before that he wanted to pin the killings on him whether he was guilty or not?

He didn't know. He forced the doubts from his mind because they made him uncomfortable.

The trail continued steadily toward Gore's place for another mile beyond the massacre site. Then, suddenly and unexpectedly, it veered back toward town.

And there was another change in it. The spacing of the horse's prints were different. Gore had speeded up. He had urged his horse from the trot he had traveled so far into a steady lope.

The trail paralleled the course of the hunters for two or three miles. Then it suddenly veered again, angling back toward that course.

Johnny felt a vague excitement rise in him. Yet he felt an unexplainable uneasiness too. What kind of second sight did he have that had made him follow the hunters' trail? What kind of premonition had made him veer aside when Gore's trail cut away?

Some strange sixth sense out of his aboriginal past, he supposed, a sense inherited along with his stoical ability to endure pain, alone with his natural ability to follow trail.

He urged his tired horse into a steady trot. He had a feeling that he was close to the answer now. And his excitement continued its steady rise.

CHAPTER 17

ANOTHER COUPLE of miles fell behind. Johnny began to wonder if this was Gore's trail after all. It could be Hunsicker's. Hunsicker had a ranch out this way, bordering on Gore's. Either Gore or Hunsicker could have left the bunch where the trail had cut away.

The land was rolling, cut by deep washes and sometimes broken by low bluffs. The trail ascended one of these bluffs and went straight to its precipitous edge.

Johnny frowned as he realized that from here he was looking straight down upon the wide, plain trail left by the men who had spent the past several days hunting him.

The trail he was following turned and continued east for half a mile. Again it stopped, and Johnny saw where the horseman had dismounted and tied his horse. Two separate piles of droppings told him the man had been here for some time.

He followed the bootprints and they led him to the edge of the bluff. There were a lot of hoofprints overlying both the horseman's trail and his bootprints, sometimes almost obscuring them. But, right at the edge of the bluff, Johnny found where the man had lain down, and he found a single, bright cartridge case.

He picked it up and put it into his pocket. Mounting again, he slid his horse off the bluff and rode to the other trail on the plain beneath.

Immediately beneath the bluff the trail stopped. From here the men had scattered and gone southward toward the bluff. At one spot there was blood in the snow and the imprint of a man's body over it.

What had happened was obvious. The man Johnny had been following, either Hunsicker or Gore, had stationed himself above the place the others would pass, and had shot one of them. It had probably happened just at dusk last night, and the ambusher had been able to escape into the night. The others had not tried to follow his trail today since they were undoubtedly convinced that Johnny had been the sniper on the bluff. But the killer had made his mistake at last. Johnny could find out easily enough who had left the others back near the Little Dry massacre site. Then he would know for sure who the killer was.

It had to be Gore, he thought. Hunsicker rarely went to his horse ranch anymore. He had a couple of men out there to look after things but the shack they lived in was certainly not the kind of place a tired man would want to go. And whoever broke away from the bunch would have to have some kind of excuse for doing so.

Gore, then. And either Hunsicker or Beeson had been shot.

Assuming that the shot had been a fatal one, and that Hunsicker was the most likely victim of the original ten, Gore, Beeson and Asbury were left alive. And if Johnny's surmises were correct, both Beeson and Asbury were in deadly peril now.

Why had Gore so suddenly gone on a killing rampage? There had to be a reason. Gore wasn't a fool and he wasn't insane. Johnny frowned thoughtfully.

Gore had cold-bloodedly planned and led the raid at the Little Dry. It wasn't generally known, of course. The nine who had ridden with him knew. Tom Ormsby knew, and through him, Johnny also knew.

Eleven men who knew Gore had planned and led the raid. Eleven who knew he had forced the others to participate, even after some of them tried to back out of it. Beeson, for example, had been knocked unconscious by Gore prior to the attack, and had thereafter had no part in it.

These were things Tom Ormsby had learned little by little over the past twenty years. They were things no other person except Johnny knew because the men who had taken part in the massacre never willingly talked about it.

Gore wanted to be governor. He probably wanted to run for the Senate after that. He might even have his eyes on the Presidency.

The fact that he had participated in a raid like the one at the Little Dry wouldn't help his political ambitions, of course, but a lot of men had fought Indians twenty years ago and not all of the battles were things of which they could be proud.

On the other hand, if Gore's political enemies knew he had planned and led the raid, that it would not have occurred without his leadership, it would be a different story altogether. Such an episode had ruined Chivington. It could ruin Gore as well and he surely knew it could. He could be made to look like a butcher instead of an Indian fighter and that would finish him.

Gore's cold-bloodedness in murdering his confederates was appalling and almost unbelievable. And yet, thought Johnny, why was it unbelievable? Twenty years ago Gore had led ten men against the village on the Little Dry. He had massacred every man, woman and child in the village mercilessly. He'd have killed Johnny had he realized that Johnny was alive.

Knowing, therefore, any one of them could tell the story that would ruin him, Gore had set out to murder his companions in the massacre. He had shot Tom, knowing Tom could tell the story too. He figured the town would catch up with Johnny and take care of him. Even if they didn't no one would believe anything Johnny said.

Cold fear touched Johnny's spine. As long as Gore was loose, Tom Ormsby was in danger. So were Asbury and Beeson, if they were indeed the remaining two.

He had to get to town. He had to talk to Tom. Somehow, he had to lay a trap for Gore because nobody, with the possible exception of Tom Ormsby, was going to believe his story now. They were all convinced he was the killer himself.

He couldn't go in daylight, though. He didn't dare. He'd be shot down before he reached Doc's office over the bank.

It would have to wait for night. And by night, Tom or any of the others might be dead.

Since there was nothing he could do immediately, he climbed the bluff again and began a large circle around the place from which the ambusher had fired the fatal shot. Sorting trails was difficult because there were so many tracks. But eventually Johnny found the ambusher's trail and followed it.

It led due south for several miles, then turned west. It headed straight toward Gore's ranch.

Johnny followed it until he came in sight of Gore's ranch house. Then he turned back toward town.

He had satisfied himself. He knew definitely that Gore was the killer and the one who had shot Tom.

Poking along, allowing his horse to graze wherever the wind or sun had uncovered the grass, he reached the vicinity of Box Elder at dusk. He sat his horse on a low bluff overlooking the town until the sky turned completely dark.

Lights winked in the windows below. He could see people moving about in the streets, both on horseback and afoot. Occasionally a wagon or buggy crawled along the street.

It looked peaceful enough. But Johnny was aware that the impression of peacefulness was misleading. Box Elder was like a powder charge, waiting only the spark of his presence to set it off. The people of Box Elder were thoroughly scared and scared people might do anything.

Cautiously he began his descent toward town. Watchfully he entered it at the lower end where the shacks of its poorer residents were, where the slaughterhouse and boneyard were, where Solomon's freight yard was.

He rode along an alley that paralleled Main, an almost intolerable tension in him now. A dog ran out, barking at him, and he softly cursed the dog to silence him. Crossing the street just below the block containing the bank, he passed within twenty feet of a man on foot and held his breath. But the man shuffled past without even looking up.

Johnny crossed the street and entered the alley that ran behind the bank. He reached the vacant lot beside it, rode toward the street, then dismounted and tied his horse beneath the stairway leading to Doc's office over the bank.

He glanced up and down the street before he climbed the stairs. He hurried up as silently as he could and ducked inside without bothering to knock.

Doc said, "Well, by God, come in!"

Johnny swung around. "How's Tom?" he asked anxiously.

"Better. Been conscious several times. But you're not doing so good. Now they say you killed Le Gros and Hunsicker."

Johnny stared at him. He felt incredibly tired and dirty. He put up a hand and felt the thin beard and crusted dirt on his face. He said harshly, "I didn't but I know who did. Can I see Tom?"

"Don't know why not. He's been worried about you. Seeing you might do him good."

Doc got up from his untidy desk and walked across the room. Johnny followed him into an adjoining room.

Tom Ormsby, looking thinner and weaker than Johnny had ever seen him, was sleeping in the bed. Doc said, "Tom. You've got a visitor."

Ormsby's eyes opened. His cracked lips made a smile. "Johnny! You all right?"

"I'm all right. How about you? When are you going to get up and get to work?"

143

"Soon as this damned sawbones will let me."
He stared at Johnny a moment, his eyes taking in
the condition of Johnny's clothes, the beard, the
dirt. . . . Johnny said, "I know who it is, Tom.
It's Gore."

Tom's eyes were incredulous. "Gore? You can't
be serious."

Johnny pulled up a chair and straddled it. "I
saw him in that bunch that was trailing me after
Le Gros was killed. They were all played out and
I suppose they wanted to bring Le Gros' body in.
Anyway, they pulled out yesterday morning and I
followed them. Near the Little Dry massacre site
one of 'em left the others and rode south. I don't
know why, but I followed him."

Ormsby's eyes studied him as he talked. "I
thought Gore was at the Capitol."

"So did I. Anyway, this trail went toward his
place for a while, then turned toward town again.
About fifteen miles short of town he shot one of
them from the top of a bluff."

"How'd he get away?"

"It must have been close to dark. And they
didn't bother to trail him. They were so sure it
was me. . . ."

"Where'd he go after that?"

"His place."

Ormsby said, "Nobody will believe you, no
matter what you say."

Johnny nodded. "I know it."

The sheriff's eyes sharpened. "What have you
got in mind?"

"There's only one reason I can think of for Gore
doing it. He doesn't want it known that he
planned and led that raid. I figure he knows it

144

would finish him politically. So he's getting rid of everyone that can point the finger at him. That's why he shot you. And it's how we can trap him, because Karl Asbury and Roy Beeson are still alive."

He swung his head and stared at Doc. "They *are* still alive, aren't they?"

Doc nodded. "Far as I know."

Johnny said, "Then they'll have to be the bait."

Tom asked, "Do me a favor, Doc?"

"If I can."

"Go down and get Karl. Bring him up here but don't tell him Johnny's here. We won't bother about Beeson right now. He's probably so goddamn scared he'd panic if he saw Johnny here. And find out if Gore's in town."

"All right." Doc put on his hat and coat and went out the door. Johnny heard him clumping heavily down the stairs.

He turned his head. "How's Gerda?"

Tom grinned. "She's fine. If I was a little younger, I'd marry her myself. That girl's got spunk."

Johnny grinned to himself, thinking of Gerda, wanting to see her. Then he frowned. He didn't know what kind of trap he could set for Gore. He hated to set it anyplace but here because that would mean Tom would be left alone. He'd need both Doc and Gerda for witnesses. Nobody was going to believe anything he said.

Tom asked, "What kind of trap have you got in mind?"

Johnny frowned thoughtfully. "I've been trying to think of something. Maybe we could get Karl up here and then, if Gore's in town, have Gerda or Doc spread the word around that Karl's doing a series of articles for his paper on the massacre, getting stories from each of the men surviving who were in on it." He grinned at Tom. "Starting with you. Maybe that would scare Gore into doing something rash. Besides, he'd figure he could get both Karl and you at the same time."

"What about Beeson?"

"He'll be safe enough. Gore isn't going to be worrying about him until after he's gotten rid of you and Karl."

Tom nodded approvingly. "Might work. If Gore's in town."

Johnny shrugged. "I guess we'll just have to hope he is."

CHAPTER 18

Doc Greene was gone about fifteen minutes. Johnny heard him clumping heavily up the stairs at the end of that time and he heard other footsteps mingling with Doc's.

He stepped across the room and positioned himself behind the door. Doc came in, followed by the tall, gaunt figure of Asbury.

Asbury said, "Doc said you wanted to see me, Tom."

"Uh huh. Johnny and me have got a plan."

Asbury swung his head nervously. He saw Johnny against the door. His eyes turned flat with sudden fear, then resignation came to them.

Johnny said softly, "You're jumping to a conclusion, Karl, just like everybody else. I'm not the killer and you don't have to be afraid of me."

"Then who is? Do you know?"

Johnny nodded. "It's Gore. I was trailing that bunch that came back to town last night. Gore cut away from them near the Little Dry and headed home. Only he didn't go right home. He speeded up and got ahead of them. He bellied down on a ridge and shot Hunsicker. It was almost dark so they couldn't trail him. And they didn't try today because they figured it was me."

Asbury's expression held outright disbelief.

"Why would Gore do it? What reason could he have for risking his career that way?"

"His political career is the reason he's doing it. Remember what happened to Chivington after the business at Sand Creek? He was finished. And Gore knows the same thing can happen to him."

"But everybody knows he was in on it. How can killing off the men who were with him change that?"

"Everybody doesn't know it was his idea. Everybody doesn't know that he planned it and led it and insisted that every one of those Indians be killed. Only Tom and I and the men who rode with him knew that."

For another instant disbelief remained in Asbury's lined face. Then he nodded, almost reluctantly. "It's possible. But good God, it's hard to believe."

"Why? You were with him at the Little Dry. You saw him in action against a bunch of surprised and helpless Indians. You know he's capable of cold-blooded murder."

Asbury studied Johnny carefully. He said, with considerable surprise, "You don't hate him at all, do you? I thought you did. All of us thought you were after revenge."

Johnny fingered the star on his shirt. He said patiently, I'm an Indian only by birth, Karl. Otherwise I'm as white as you are. Tom raised me and I've lived in Box Elder all my life. If I hate Gore at all it's because he's a killer and I'm Tom's deputy. Now will you help us set a trap for him?"

Doc said, "He's in town, Johnny. He's down at the Buckhorn."

Asbury asked nervously, "What kind of trap?"

Johnny grinned faintly. "Doc's going down to the Buckhorn for a nightcap like he usually does. Chances are somebody will ask him about Tom and he'll say that you came up to talk to Tom about some stories you're going to do on the Massacre. He'll say that because you're with Tom he got a chance to leave for a while.

"And that will bring Gore up here. Is that it?"

"Exactly. Only we'll be ready for him. Doc will come on back, and we'll have Gerda here. That ought to be enough witnesses to hang him higher than a kite."

"What if? . . ." Asbury's face was a little pale.

Johnny said, "If we don't catch him, you're in a hell of a lot more danger than you will be while we're catching him."

Asbury nodded reluctatly. "I guess you're right. " He looked at Tom, as though for reassurance. Tom nodded.

Johnny said, "Doc, on your way to the Buckhorn, will you stop by the hotel and have Gerda come up here?"

"Sure Johnny."

"And after you've dropped your little bombshell at the Buckhorn, finish your drink and come on back."

"All right." Doc put on his hat and went out. Johnny pulled his revolver from its holster and handed it to Tom. He went out into the other room and got Doc's old hunting rifle from its rack. He got a handful of cartridges after rummaging through Doc's desk, then went in where Asbury and Tom were punching shells into the gun. He said, "Karl, pull up a chair beside the bed and get a paper and pencil out."

"Where are you going to be?"

"I'll stay out there in Doc's office. I'll get over behind the door. I doubt if Gore will see me. He'll be too interested in you and Tom."

Karl grinned shakily. "I feel like a sitting duck."

Johnny grinned back. "You're not even a real live duck. You're a decoy."

Asbury got a chair and dragged it to the bedside. He sat down and got out a pad and pencil. Tom's eyes rested steadily on Johnny's face. But they no longer held the slightest doubt.

Johnny heard steps on the outside stairway and went quickly to Doc's office. He reached the door before he realized that the footsteps did not belong to a man. They were too quick, too light.

The door opened and Gerda came in. When she saw Johnny, her eyes filled with tears. She ran to his arms. "Johnny! Oh Johnny, I was so scared!"

He said, "It's almost over now. We know who the killer is."

"Who is it?"

"Gore." Quickly he told her what he had discovered and what he believed. He said, "You get in there with Tom and Karl, but sit behind the door. Gore will probably start shooting the minute he comes in."

"Where will you be?"

"Right here."

"No Johnny! He'll. . . ."

"He won't do anything. Now go do what I told you to. A good squaw never argues with her buck."

She looked into his face for a long moment.

Then she said, "Yes Johnny," and left him and went into the other room. For a moment all was quiet.

Johnny heard more footsteps on the stairs. Doc sounded tired, he thought. He was practically dragging up the stairs.

He heard a hand on the door. He turned his head....

The door stood open, hiding whoever stood behind it from his eyes. He glanced into the bedroom. Tom was staring toward the doorway. His hand was fumbling frantically beneath the covers. Asbury's head was turned....

Caught off guard by his belief the footsteps had belonged to Doc, Johnny suddenly realized it was Gore standing behind the door. It was Gore and he had a gun in his hand, a gun that was pointed at Asbury and Tom....

He threw himself against the door. He heard a muffled curse. A gun discharged thunderously....

Gore stumbled heavily across the room. He slammed against the wall, swinging, bringing his gun to bear.

His eyes blazed with fury, with hate, with the knowledge that he had been trapped. Johnny, also off balance, yanked the awkward rifle around, thumbing back the hammer as he did.

Gore's gun steadied. Again sound filled the room, horrible in this place that had known only Doc's lifelong attempts to ease pain and to cure sickness.

Gore's bullet clanged harshly on the barrel of Johnny's rifle, tore into the wooden stock and shattered it, missing his hand but filling his forearm with splinters.

Johnny was caught momentarily by surprise. The gun was useless now. And Gore's was steadying for another shot.

Johnny leaped aside like a cat, then changed directions and lunged at Gore, using the rifle as a club. His hands were numb from the bullet's shock, and he could scarcely feel with them.

Gore fired twice, in rapid succession. Both shots missed. And Johnny saw something in Gore's eyes . . . something he had seen in other faces recently. Gore couldn't understand Johnny's failure to hate and because he didn't understand he refused to believe. He was convinced that Johnny was now trying to kill him because of what had happened at Little Dry.

The rifle swung like a club, but just before it struck, Johnny pulled it, lessening its impact deliberately. It struck Gore's head, but not with the killing force with which it had started to swing.

Gore collapsed, his gun clattering from his hand. Johnny lowered the clubbed rifle, leaned against the wall and rubbed his splinter-filled forearm.

He heard someone in the doorway behind him and swung his head warily. But it was only Doc.

Johnny said, "He isn't dead. He's knocked out but he isn't dead. He'll live to go to trail."

For the first time since all this had started with De Loach's death, he was sure of himself. Before he had wondered if something deeply hidden inside of him didn't hate as they said it did, and thirst for a long-delayed revenge.

But now he knew. He didn't hate because of Little Dry. He wasn't a Cheyenne brave. He was what Tom Ormsby had made him, what his environment had shaped of him. He was a lawman. He was Tom's deputy.

He pushed himself away from the wall. Doc knelt beside the prostrate body of Gore. Looking up he said, "He'll come out of it in a few minutes with nothing worse than a bad headache."

Johnny went into the other room. He saw Gerda, standing white-faced, frightened, but strong and straight. Her eyes looked into his as though they would never look away.

Johnny looked at Tom, and at Asbury. He said, "Karl, you've got a better story now than you came here for."

Asbury stood up. "I've never gotten out an extra in my life, but I'm getting one out tonight. I want this whole damned county to know what kind of a deputy they've got."

Johnny grinned at Gerda. "Looks like you won't have to live in a tipi after all."

For an instant she stared at him. Then, both laughing and crying, she came to his arms with an eagerness that made his blood race in spite of his weariness.

Tom whistled. "I think you two had better get married tomorrow."

Johnny pulled away, as shaken as he had ever been in his life. "Seems like an awful long time to wait."

Out in the other room, Gore groaned. Johnny went out there and helped him to his feet. He pushed him out the door, staying close behind. Asbury followed anxiously.

There was a crowd at the bottom of the stairs,

looking up. Asbury stood on the landing while Johnny followed Gore down the stairs. He yelled, "Gore's the killer we've all been looking for! Johnny set a trap for him and caught him when he tried to kill Tom and me. Now get out of the way and let Tom's deputy take him down to the jail. There'll be an extra on the street in an hour and you can read all about it then."

The crowd made way. Johnny heard Asbury tell someone to take his horse to the stable. He followed Gore down the street to the jail, locked him in, built a fire and stared for a moment at the couch. Then he crossed the room and laid down on it. He was asleep almost before his eyes were closed.

He never heard the commotion caused by the release of Karl Asbury's extra edition. He didn't hear Gore, yelling in his cell. He slept as though he was dead until nine o'clock the next morning, when Gerda wakened him by bringing breakfast both for him and for Bradford Gore.

He carried it back to Gore, unlocked the door and put it on the floor. Gore sat on his cot, glowering.

He returned to Gerda, feeling better than he had in days. Much of the soreness was gone from his body and he felt rested. He said, "Go on back to the hotel. I'll go over home and clean up. I'll meet you there in an hour."

He kissed her, not missing the high color in her face, the shine in her eyes. She left, and he ate the breakfast she had brought. Finished, he locked up and walked to the little house in which he and Tom Ormsby lived. He'd stay here in Box Elder until Tom was well, he thought. After that. . . . Well, there ought to be some place where he and Gerda could live.

The hate was gone from the people of the town. They no longer thought he was a murderer. But he was still Indian. He was still a race apart. They'd never let him forget it, and they wouldn't let Gerda forget it, either.

He bathed and shaved and put on clean clothes. He walked back to Main and along it to the hotel. People looked at him and looked away. Or they spoke, almost grudgingly.

It wouldn't work, staying here. He'd tried, but it wouldn't work. Next time something came up . . . next time there was doubt . . . it would be the same thing all over again.

Gerda and Asbury were waiting for him. Doc said, "Tom sends his congratulations and good wishes Johnny."

Johnny nodded, his eyes on Gerda. If he had Gerda nothing else would matter to him.

The four walked along the street toward the tiny frame church at its upper end. Where the walk entered the churchyard by a neat white gate, Johnny stopped suddenly.

He hadn't thought anyone would come. He stared at the crowd waiting in the churchyard.

They were all here, the ones who had wanted to take him out of the sheriff's office forcibly, the ones who had chased him through the mountains for so many days. They shuffled their feet and looked at the ground like boys caught playing hooky from school. And he understood something he had not understood before.

They had avoided his eyes—they had spoken in

what seemed a grudging manner because they were ashamed. They were still ashamed. Of their prejudice, of jumping to the conclusion that he was guilty because they understood hatred, because they understood revenge.

But now. . . . A few of them looked up and met his glance determindedly. And there was nothing but friendliness in their eyes.

He had made a place for himself after all. There was no longer any need to go away. Johnny suddenly felt warm, and good.

Karl, walking ahead of him and Gerda, stopped on the church steps and turned. He said in a voice loud enough for all to hear: "Tom told me just a few minutes ago that he was going to retire next year. I'd like to ask Johnny something before we all go inside so I can put it in the paper when the wedding's over."

Johnny stared at him puzzledly. Asbury asked, "Will you run for sheriff next year when Tom retires? I think there's a good many people here who would like to vote for you."

Johnny turned his head and looked at the faces of the crowd. He looked down into Gerda's shining eyes.

He grinned, slowly and comfortably. He said, "Well now, I just believe I will, I like it here."

Still smiling, he turned and walked with Gerda into the tiny church. The townspeople filed in silently after them.